Yellow
with Black Spots

Yolanda Powell

CONTENTS

1

Arrival

The coach pulled into Place de la République and swung round in front of a large café to disgorge its passengers. Katherine stepped out into the early evening air and joined the queue for the luggage, which was being hauled out by the driver and then dumped unceremoniously on the pavement. A tall, thin, white-haired man stood up from one of the tables at the café and waved to her. This was Patrick, an old friend of her father's whom she had met briefly a couple of times when he had been in England.

'Katherine, welcome to Paris. Let's have a drink – I should think you're ready for one,' said Patrick, as he stooped to kiss her on both cheeks.

'Thank you, I'd love one.'

Patrick and Katherine settled down at the table and a waiter took their order.

'How is Henry?' Patrick enquired.

'Oh, he's fine. He said to tell you that he's started on your book at last.'

Katherine's father had received Patrick's manuscript, all 823 pages of it, several weeks back but had lacked the courage to open it until a couple of days before Katherine's departure. Patrick had a tendency to write very long, rambling diatribes about government institutions, which he then inflicted on Henry to review with the aim of finding a publisher. The latest opus concerned the corruption at the heart of the United Nations. Henry was not hopeful of finding it a home.

Katherine had arrived late in Paris. The exchange organisation had been very slow to confirm that she had a post as an assistante d'anglais and it had looked at one time that she would have to return to Oxford to complete her final year. So, it was nearly mid-September when she boarded her student flight.

She had been to France only once before, in the summer before going up to college. She had passed through Paris on that visit but that was all. Paris was almost as exotic to Katherine as the Amazon might be to today's well-travelled student. To be independent – of home, of college, of friends – for a whole year was daunting and exciting. It seemed to Katherine that she would be able to sort herself out once and for all, decide who she was and what she wanted.

She had hesitated at first over whether to apply as an assistante. Most of her fellow students had not applied and the college was not keen, so, ever susceptible to influence from others, she had begun to question whether the break from her degree course would be of any real value. But, in the end, Katherine had applied and been rewarded with Paris, rather than by a post in a dull provincial town, such as the one Janice had landed.

The student flight from Ashford was uneventful but a little bumpy, and Katherine was pleased when the plane touched down on firm ground. The coach journey from Beauvais into Paris through green but unexciting countryside took longer than the flight and, by the time she had arrived at Place de la République to be greeted by Patrick, Katherine was feeling tired and grubby.

She drank her wine slowly, realising that it would go to her head if she did not. Patrick drank his rather faster and ordered himself another.

'I expect you could do with something to eat. We'll check you into your hotel and go and have a meal. Tomorrow I'm afraid you will have to move to the other side of town to somewhere cheaper, as it may take a while for you to find somewhere to live,' said Patrick. 'Of course, I should have been delighted to have you stay with me, but my flat is much too small – a real bachelor pad.'

'Oh, no problem. I'm just very grateful to you for arranging anything at all, it's very kind of you.'

'Nonsense, I am only too delighted to help.'

After both had finished their drinks, Patrick paid and they left for the hotel, taking a taxi for the short journey to a side street just south of the river.

Katherine's room looked comfortable if crowded, with floral wallpaper covering not just the walls but also the ceiling, chintz curtains and bedcover, and a profusion of lamps and a cosy though old-fashioned en-suite bathroom. Looking out of the window, she was delighted to be presented by a magnificent view of Notre Dame. She dropped her cases to the floor and fished out her washbag. A few minutes later, she went down the ancient, winding staircase to where Patrick was waiting in the lobby.

Patrick took Katherine to a local restaurant that he knew well.

'Monsieur Holgate, how nice to see you,' beamed the maitre d' as he led the small party to a corner table.

'Thank you, Georges,' replied Patrick, 'It's a pleasure to be back

– I really should come more often, but I just don't seem to find the time. Still, here we are this evening. What do you recommend?'

'For you, Monsieur, I would suggest the goat's cheese salad followed by wild mushroom risotto. For mademoiselle, what about our home-made terrine and then perhaps our chicken à la basquaise - with red peppers and tomato?'

'That sounds splendid. Agreed, Katherine?'

'Yes, great.'

Wine, water and bread were placed quickly on the table and then Patrick talked at her rather than to her while they ate their way through a simple but satisfying meal.

Katherine was glad to return to the hotel afterwards and sank down on the bed while the bathwater was running. A warm soak relaxed her tired body and she climbed into bed full of optimism, a feeling possibly enhanced by the quantities of wine that she and Patrick had consumed during the previous hour and a half.

The next morning, Patrick came by and paid her bill. He put her into a taxi, pressing the money for the fare into her hands. Giving directions to the taxi driver, he waved her away before turning back towards the Metro. As he made his own way home, Patrick reflected that Katherine was going to have to change quite a lot if she was to enjoy her time in his Paris. She seemed intelligent enough but her shapeless clothes, epitomising the English lack of style, and her excess weight told against her. He wanted to help her settle in, for Henry's sake, but it was difficult to see how she would fit in with his particular crowd.

The change of hotels brought Katherine down with a bump. The Hotel Tour Eiffel was dark, shabby and uninviting. The man behind the reception desk looked her up and down with an expression that hovered between disdain and lechery. She filled in the hotel occupancy form and he handed her the key to her room on the second floor. At least there was a lift, though it cranked and whirred into action at an alarmingly painful and slow rate.

Her room was surprisingly large – it even had two beds in it - but the furnishings were drab and worn. There was a wardrobe, a table and a chair, an old-fashioned telephone. The wallpaper was yellowed with age, the dark-green curtains felt strangely plastic to the touch and the shower cubicle was only just large enough to wash in; she would have to towel down in the bedroom. Still, it was only for a few days.

2

Education

The lycée was round the corner from St Paul metro station in the centre of Paris. It was a single-sex school, taking girls from the ages of 15 to 18 or 19. Its main buildings dated from the eighteenth century and their elegant classical façade seemed to embody the aesthetic appeal and refined grace of Paris. Katherine had never seen a school like it before. Her own, girls-only grammar school, a rectangular 1920s institution sited in the middle of playing fields and standing aloof from its surroundings, bore no comparison with this crowded, urban society.

'Hello, my name is Katherine Stewart and I am the new assistante d'anglais,' Katherine told the secretary in the school office. 'Where should I go?'

'Ah, you need to see Madame Grondin. I'll send someone to find her.'

Madame Grondin arrived a few minutes later, a short, middle-aged woman, her greying hair pulled up into a bun, tweedy clothes, an air of excitable energy. She could have stepped out of an Agatha Christie novel – a Gallic version of Miss Marple.

'You must be Katherine,' she gushed in English. 'Come, let us go to the café and discuss what you will do.'

Madame Grondin led Katherine out of the school and round the corner. 'We shall go to Bar Raynaud. Perhaps you would like something to go with the coffee?'

Madame bustled her way into a patisserie next door to the café and bought two chaussons aux pommes, apple turnovers.

Once installed at a table, Madame Grondin carefully unwrapped the precious packages, ordered coffee and advised Katherine that the proprietor was quite happy if people brought in a pastry to eat.

'He does not mind because he does not serve food. But you cannot do this in every bar.'

The chausson was delicious but messy, and little pastry crumbs and flakes soon littered the table.

'Where are you staying?'

'In a hotel near the Eiffel Tower but I can't stay there too long.'

'No, of course not. I shall ask Mademoiselle Mercier if she has any ideas. You see, it can be difficult to find places to live in Paris. We do not have the same custom of sharing flats as you do in England so finding somewhere affordable may take some time. You could try the notice-board at the American Church or at the Alliance Française – foreign students are more likely to be looking to share. You do not need to come back here until Wednesday, so you have five days to try and sort something out."

'I see,' Katherine replied, disappointed that the school had no ready-made system for helping its helpers.

'Now, as to your classes, you will be taking several groups of girls for conversation and I shall also ask you to record passages for us to use in the language laboratory. Last year, we had an American girl. She was very nice but it will be good for our girls to hear English spoken with the proper accent.

'I think that you may have four or so classes. The brightest are those in deuxième, I think you will enjoy teaching them. The girls you will teach in final year, Terminale, are the ones who are taking vocational courses, typing, shorthand, that kind of thing. They are not very academic, I'm afraid, but most of them are quite sweet.'

'We do not have school on Wednesday afternoon but we do have classes on Saturday mornings. You will find our system very different from what you are used to. You see, if our girls have no classes, they do not need to be in school – and neither do you. We do not have many extra-curricular activities; we're not so keen on clubs as the English. You should have plenty of time to yourself for your own studies.'

'I see,' said Katherine again. She wondered how she was going to cope – girls in Terminale would be almost as old as she was.

3

Lodgings

Searching for digs proved time-consuming and unrewarding. The notice-board at the American Church was bereft of offers, probably as a result of Katherine's late arrival in Paris – most students and foreign visitors had already sorted out their accommodation. The small ads in the newspapers contained little that Katherine could even begin to contemplate. On her salary of 1,000 francs a month, she could barely afford even the tiniest of studios. She visited a couple that were on offer but one was a good fifteen minute walk from the nearest metro station and was approached through narrow winding, shadowy streets lined with tiny, badly-lit bars blaring out Middle Eastern music. Katherine did not feel secure visiting it even in daylight. The other studio was filthy and the landlord too keen to get her to sign.

In a fit of dedication, Katherine signed up for a French language course at the Alliance, though the notice-board was as unhelpful as the one at the church. Following the entrance tests, she was disappointed to be placed not in the top class but the next level down. Her fellow classmates were a mix of Japanese, assorted Europeans, an American and, to her surprise, several North Africans. She had not expected people who were, presumably, largely brought up with the French language to be enrolled in classes.

Two Algerians latched on to Katherine very quickly. They sat either side of her in class and insisted on eating lunch with her in the canteen. They followed her out of class into the street. She found that she could not avoid them. After the third lesson had followed the same pattern, she resolved somewhat drastically to forego her fee, which she could not really afford, and not to return to the Alliance. She would sign up at the Sorbonne instead.

Katherine explained her difficulties in finding suitable accommodation to Madame Grondin. She could not afford to stay much longer in her hotel but she had found nowhere else to stay. Madame had a word with Mademoiselle Mercier who offered to put Katherine up for a short while in her own flat, which was in the Rue du Faubourg St Honoré.

With great relief, Katherine checked out of the Hôtel Tour Eiffel and moved in with the head of the English department. The flat was tiny, in estate agents' parlance bijou. There were just two rooms, a small kitchen and bathroom. The living room was over-stuffed, like a Victorian parlour. Its dark green walls were covered in small oil paintings in gilded frames, which looked down on a sofa and two armchairs, all covered in floral upholstery, a sideboard groaning with knick-knacks and a matching pair of glass-fronted wooden bookcases. A circular, highly polished table sat on a Persian rug between the chairs. A small writing desk, several high-backed dining chairs, a couple of table lamps and a tall standard lamp completed the furnishings.

'I am afraid there is only one bedroom,' said Mademoiselle Mercier, 'so, I hope you will not mind sleeping on the sofa. I think it will be quite comfortable for a short stay.'

'No, of course not,' replied Katherine. 'It's very kind of you to put me up.'

For the next few days, Katherine doubled her efforts to find somewhere else to live but the situation seemed increasingly hopeless. Eventually, Mademoiselle Mercier mentioned that an acquaintance of hers, who was very active in the Cercle Franco-Britannique, was looking for someone to give her boys English conversation classes.

'She has a room available at a very low rent. Perhaps you would like to see it?'

Mademoiselle Mercier made the arrangements and the following day Katherine made her way to the Rue de Rivoli.

The old-fashioned lift, a wrought-iron and glass cage that groaned marginally less than the one at the hotel, took Katherine up to the fourth floor and the Duval apartment. Madame Duval was waiting in a very large drawing room that could have swallowed up Mademoiselle Mercier's flat with room to spare. Along one side were three tall French windows framed by heavy silk brocade curtains that fell in luxuriant folds to the polished wooden parquet floor. Katherine noted three different Persian carpets and lost count of the number of occasional tables dotted around the room, each with its own lamp sporting a ruched silk shade.

As indicated by Madame, Katherine sat on a sofa, separated from her inquisitor by a coffee table embellished with a huge flower arrangement.

'So, Mademoiselle Mercier tells me that you are at Oxford,' began Madame Duval in an almost perfect English accent.

'Yes, I've been there for two years.'

'Good, and what does your father do?'

'He's mainly a writer of fiction, magazine stories, that kind of thing.'

'Oh, really, any magazines I would know?'

'Mainly women's mags, you know, Woman's Realm, She, that kind of thing.'

'I see, I cannot say I have read any of those.'

There wasn't much to be said in reply so Katherine stayed silent. Madame Duval stared thoughtfully at the flowers in the vase, her clasped hands resting on her lap, the sunlight catching on an exceptionally large diamond ring that glinted furiously at the slightest movement. Katherine shifted in her seat, wondering whether there were any questions she should be asking in turn. Before she could think of any, Madame Duval spoke.

'Well, I expect you would like to see the room.'

Katherine followed Madame Duval as she moved briskly through the apartment towards the kitchen, out through a door and up two flights of stairs to where the chambres de bonne (maids' rooms) huddled below the eaves.

The room was small, very small. The door opened to reveal a narrow bed to the right and a writing desk cum chest of drawers to the left. Next to the desk was a thin wooden wardrobe and beyond that a single free-standing electric ring. A small wall-hung washbasin filled the gap to the external wall. The dormer set into the roof was taller than Katherine and through the window she could see only sky. To the right, a school-style radiator occupied most of the space between the foot of the bed and the end wall. Apart from a small mirror, there was nothing on the pale, sludge-pink walls.

Madame Duval led Katherine back down the stairs into the apartment.

'Well,' she said, 'as you can see, the room is small but clean and, if you want a shower, just knock on the back door of the apartment. The rent is only 250 francs per month, but I should wish you to give English conversation lessons to my two sons once a week. I will pay you eight francs per lesson. I am sure you will not find a better deal. What do you say?'

Katherine really wanted to refuse. The room was tiny and Madame Duval was quite intimidating. Katherine had not met the boys to whom she was supposed to give lessons and she had no idea whether or not the rent was a good deal, though it seemed very reasonable. On the other hand, getting to school would be incredibly easy and the area was very smart. Most importantly, she knew she had to find an alternative to Mademoiselle Mercier's flat. She had found nowhere else and was not sure she could handle too many more evenings of polite conversation. It would do as a stop-gap.

'Yes, Madame, that would be fine.'

'Good. You may move in as soon as you wish. Please use the backstairs when you return. The concierge will show you. I suggest you come and see me on Monday evening and we will arrange your first lessons with Yves and André.'

Madame Duval took Katherine back through the salon, back through the vast, polished hall and out to the lift. The iron cage rumbled to a stop, Katherine got in and said goodbye to Madame Duval, who turned smartly into the apartment and closed the door.

Back at Mademoiselle Mercier's, Katherine packed her cases and waited for the teacher to return. Mademoiselle was clearly relieved that the girl had decided to take the chambre de bonne and wished her well. She did not protest when Katherine said she was thinking of moving straightaway. As it was a Friday,

Mademoiselle Mercier was going to her pavillon in the country for the weekend, so if Katherine left at the same time, that would be a neat and tidy resolution.

Katherine struggled down the stairs with her cases. She thought briefly about hailing a taxi but quickly dismissed the idea. She had not yet been paid and her money was very low. It seemed ridiculously extravagant to pay for a taxi to take her in a straight line to the apartment building. Taking the metro was not an option because the railway workers were on strike. She started to walk purposefully along the Rue du Faubourg St Honoré. It was hard work, one of the cases was very heavy indeed and the pavement was very narrow. She stopped and started, trying not to bump into people as they hurried by and swapping the cases over at increasingly short intervals. She had gone perhaps no more than 100 metres when she ground to a halt. Weight training would have come in useful.

4

Rue de Rivoli

'Mademoiselle, may I help you?'

Katherine turned around to face a young man, tall and thin with dark hair and a lazy eye. He was quite dark, possibly north African. Her experience to date with north Africans had not been good. She felt she should refuse but she also knew that she was tired and was not at all sure that she would be able to make it on her own.

'That would be kind,' she replied weakly.

The youth picked up both cases and walked along by her side, smiling cheerfully and asking where she was going. She explained that she was moving into a chambre de bonne on the Rue de Rivoli.

'*Chouette*,' he replied. 'Allow me to introduce myself - my name is Jacky and, as it happens, the Rue de Rivoli is on my way to work, so that's just fine.'

Once arrived at the building, Katherine hesitated. She did

not really want the young man to come any further and she felt vaguely embarrassed at the thought of the concierge's seeing him but she had the problem of negotiating the stairs.

Katherine knocked on the concierge's door. The concierge was sitting watching television. She stirred reluctantly and pushed open the top half of the door, leaning over the bottom half, like a horse leaning out of its stall.

'Yes?'

'Good day, Madame, my name is Katherine Stewart and I am renting a chambre de bonne from Madame Duval. Could you show me the way, please?'

Madame la concierge grunted, picked up some keys and came out of her room. She had dark, straggly hair, thick black eyebrows and a smear of red lipstick on her lips. Her long skirt was largely hidden by an apron and her hands were reddened and rough. She glanced at the young man carrying the cases but made no comment as she locked her door and then led the duo through the courtyard, past the rubbish bins and towards the back stairs in the far left-hand corner.

'Here, Mademoiselle, is the key to your room. You must take your rubbish to those bins over there. If you have any post, you may collect it from me. Anything else?'

'No, Madame, thank you.'

Jacky began to haul the cases up the stairs before Katherine could decide whether or not he should. The chambres de bonne were six floors up, which meant 12 turns of the winding, steep wooden staircase. By the time they reached the top floor, both were a little out of breath – Jacky because he had been carrying the cases, Katherine because she was quite unfit. She could feel her heart racing and wondered idly whether climbing up and down the stairs would help her lose weight.

Katherine turned the key in the door of what was now her room and paused awkwardly. Jacky pushed her cases into the room and grinned.

'I must go to work now,' he said. 'Would you like to meet up later? We could go for a coffee or whatever you like.'

'I don't know. I need to sort my things out.'

'Well, tomorrow then. I will come by at four o'clock and meet you downstairs.'

Katherine couldn't see the harm in one drink, after all Jacky had been very kind. She agreed.

After Jacky had left, Katherine sat down on the bed and wondered how she was going to live in this tiny space. Her trunk would arrive in a week or two with most of her books and more clothes. How would they all fit in? She turned wearily to the first case and opened it on the floor, emptying the contents onto the bed first so that she could close up the case and move it out of the way under the bed. The wardrobe had a few metal hangers on which she placed two dresses and a jacket. She put her shoes at the bottom of the wardrobe and her underwear into one of the drawers of the bureau.

Paper, pens and her diary found a place in the bureau. Her washbag she stuck under the washbasin, next to a small saucepan and frying pan that were already there.

The second, bigger case that had caused her so much difficulty contained sweaters and trousers, books and her winter coat. She found spaces for these plus a small album of photographs, some make-up, and a magazine she had bought while at Mademoiselle Mercier's. She balanced the books and a portable radio her mother had given her on a small shelf above the radiator. Finally, she laid a nightdress on the bed. It was dark now and Katherine had turned on both the central light and the lamp by her bed.

She gazed at the nightdress and asked herself yet again why she had bought it. It was not nightwear, it was lingerie – a long, floaty concoction of pale blue chiffon with layers of skirt and a button-up front. The sleeves were long, puffing out into the cuffs, and the neckline had a small collar. It was meant to make its wearer feel romantic, Hollywood, sophisticated, grown-up – like Grace Kelly in Rear Window - but Katherine knew that it made her feel fat, short, uncomfortable. But it had seemed so feminine – and Katherine had desperately wanted to feel feminine and desirable. It would fit much better when she had lost some weight.

Katherine then realised that she needed to go to the loo. Madame Duval had indicated the lavatory at the end of the corridor at the top of the stairs when she showed her the room. Katherine stepped out, carefully closing the door behind her, walked to the end of the corridor and opened the door. Realising that she would have to close the door for the light to come on, Katherine went in and locked the door. A bare light bulb flickered into life and Katherine saw to her horror that the loo was a squat-splat – two tiled footplates either side of a hole over which you have to squat to perform. The loo was moderately clean at this time although it smelt unmistakably of excrement. A small roll of scratchy paper hung off the wall. Katherine was pleased she only wanted to pee.

5

Jacky

The next afternoon, Jacky was lolling patiently outside the door when Katherine came out, half hoping that he would not be there. He suggested they go to the café on the corner. They sat inside at a banquette and ordered - an express for him, a grand crème for her. From the ensuing conversation, Katherine gathered that Jacky was a painter and decorator, who moonlighted several nights a week as a kitchen hand. He lived outside Paris in one of the new towns; his mother was French and his father Algerian.

They were not well matched. His education was clearly minimal and his tastes and interests unlikely to coincide with hers. But he was very polite and, from what she had seen, had a good body. Katherine was still suffering badly from the break-up with her last boyfriend, Duncan. His treatment of her had left her very insecure and convinced that no-one would find her attractive. This young man appeared to have no doubts about her appeal. She would take what she could get.

The conversation continued aimlessly for an hour or so and then Katherine asked Jacky if he would like to see her room.

After that, they went out four or five times. He took her to the cinema and to a Moroccan restaurant where she ate couscous for the first time – and was violently sick afterwards. They also went to a jazz club called Le Chat qui saute. The club was in the basement of an old building in the Latin Quarter. Dark, low-ceilinged and smoke-filled, with tables jostling together, the club met all Katherine's pre-conceived ideas of what such clubs should be and she enjoyed the visit, even if she put to the back of her mind that she would have enjoyed it more if her companion had been different. The vast gap between their education and backgrounds rendered most conversations meaningless – she realised that she should finish with Jacky but was afraid of the loneliness that would inevitably follow.

On the plus side, he was good in bed. Once she got used to the faint smell of paint and turpentine on his hands and body, she enjoyed their times in bed more than any other aspect of their relationship. He was young and very fit – and more experienced than she was or Duncan had been. He found ways of bringing her pleasure that she hadn't even imagined before. He was completely without guile and would grin at her afterwards, looking at her lopsidedly with his lazy eye and stating quite simply, 'I'm pretty depraved, aren't I?'

One of the reasons that Katherine began to tire of the relationship, although not one that she was too willing to admit to herself, was that he was North African. Paris had thousands of North African workers from France's former colonies – Morocco, Tunisia and Algeria – and it seemed to Katherine that they all chose to zero in on her every time she went outside. If she went to post a letter, she could be sure that at least one would either call after her suggestively or come up to her and try to engage her in conversation. It was quite clear that sex was being asked for or at least hinted at – and Katherine took a while to perfect the cold stare and withering put-down to cut any conversation short.

Many of the North Africans were poor. They did all the menial jobs that the French did not want to do. They were metro cleaners, road cleaners, painters, bus drivers, factory workers. A few worked as waiters. They lived in cramped run-down apartments with sometimes as many as six sharing one room and rotating beds by working different shifts. Katherine knew this because one day Jacky had taken her to see some friends in a cheerless suburb to the north of the centre. Grey sheets covered three flimsy campbeds in a room that was perhaps ten feet square. Four young men were there when they arrived and Katherine could sense that Jacky was showing them his trophy white female even if she could not understand the conversation. When they left, she found herself scratching her skin – the thought of bed bugs and fleas was running through her head.

Fate dictated the end of the affair when Jacky took her to Chartier, a fabulous left-over from the fin de siècle with its wood-panelled walls, large mirrors and waiters dressed in traditional long white aprons wrapped around their waists. The tables were covered in paper, allowing customers and waiters alike to tot up the bill on the table covering before it was whisked away and new paper laid for the next diners. The food was typical – eggs mayonnaise, tomatoes in vinaigrette, steak, crème caramel – and very cheap.

Katherine enjoyed the meal, the bustle and noise, the slightly offhand manner of the waiters, the absolute Frenchness of it all. But as she and Jacky emerged into the street, they bumped into Patrick. He was politeness itself but Katherine knew immediately that he did not approve.

He was very firm when next she saw him.

'Katherine, you cannot, no you must not, go out with that young man. He is completely unsuitable. What on earth would Henry say if he knew?'

She knew he was right. Two days later she finished with Jacky.

6

Teaching

Katherine discovered that she enjoyed teaching. At first, she had felt very awkward standing in front of a group of girls and attempting to draw English conversation out of them but as the term progressed she relaxed into her work and was pleased to note the progress that some of her students were making. She was also flattered to be asked to make recordings of well-known texts for the department to use in general and she spent several happy hours reading out loud from Dickens and Austen or Hemingway and Fitzgerald.

The least responsive class were the girls in Terminale, who tended to smile vacuously at her as she spoke to them, stare at their beautifully-painted finger nails and then make half-hearted attempts to formulate whole sentences. These were the girls who were destined to become secretaries rather than go on to university and their classes focused primarily on acquiring skills, such as shorthand and office management. English was seen as a passport to better-paid jobs and, so, these 18 and 19 year olds should have been motivated to try harder but, somehow, Katherine couldn't find the right approach to inspire them. She despaired that they would ever be able to do more than remark on the weather.

The girls in deuxième were quite different. They were a more challenging group to handle because they were brighter and easily bored. But they had a great sense of fun and curiosity and Katherine enjoyed finding topics that they would want to discuss. It did not take too long before one of the girls suggested that, as they had no classes before their English lesson, it might be fun to hold the class in a local café. Katherine allowed herself to be persuaded and from then on they met in a café on Rue St Antoine. Naturally enough, in such surroundings, the conversations often ended up as French lessons for Katherine as much as English lessons for her girls.

7

Bath time

A couple of days after moving in, Katherine plucked up the courage to knock on the back door of the Duval apartment, towel and soap in hand.

'Yes?' enquired the white-jacketed man who answered her knock.

'Madame Duval said I could take a shower in the flat. I'm staying upstairs,' explained Katherine hesitantly.

Unsmiling, the man opened the door and let Katherine in. They were in the kitchen, a vast room with copper and steel pots and pans hanging gleaming from the ceiling, at least two cookers and what seemed to Katherine to be acres of work surface. A woman she took to be the cook was in a far corner peeling vegetables. The man directed Katherine to an alcove on the left.

'The shower is there,' he said.

And so it was. A square, plastic shower tray draped in almost translucent plastic shower curtains. A wall jutted out in front of the shower giving a marginal degree of privacy. A wooden chair stood next to the shower and Katherine placed her towel on it. She felt both angry and embarrassed. In an apartment where there must be at least three bathrooms, she was having to take a shower in the kitchen. She turned on the water, which shot out noisily from the shower head.

Having removed her clothes, Katherine tested the water. It was at best lukewarm. Stepping under it, Katherine shivered involuntarily. As she washed, the temperature fluctuated between tepid and chill. She showered very quickly, towelled herself dry and dressed as fast as she could. Taking her belongings from the chair, she let herself out to the complete indifference of the staff moving about the kitchen. She fled upstairs and slumped on the bed.

8

Do you speak English?

Katherine had prepared carefully for the first conversation lesson with Yves, the elder of the Duval boys, but she had not prepared for his attitude.

'I don't know why we're bothering,' were Yves' opening remarks.

'We often visit England and I already speak English very well. How are you going to improve my English?'

'I don't know – but the deal is I give you lessons so we'd better get on with it,' replied Katherine, taken aback by the unexpected attack.

Yves was blond, blue-eyed and dressed in a sweater and jeans that had undoubtedly cost more than Katherine would earn in several months. He was fifteen, cock-sure and resentful of having to waste his time with this dull English girl. The lesson did not go well and Katherine was not looking forward to her conversation with André.

'Well, when shall we have our next lesson?' she asked as brightly as possible at the end of the allotted-half-hour.

'Oh, I really don't know. You'd better call next week and we'll see when is convenient.'

'Fine, we'll sort something out when I come for André's lesson.'

'I suppose so. Goodbye.' Yves left Katherine in the study where they had been sitting across a small table next to a window. She gathered up her books and walked back through the apartment to the kitchen, where she let herself out. She wondered whether Madame Duval knew how rude her son was and considered having a word about him to her. She decided, on reflection, that it was unlikely that Madame would welcome such criticism and, so, she did nothing.

9

Chez Patrick

Patrick lived in a small apartment in the 16th arrondissement, a smart part of town, the Holland Park of Paris, and it was quite surprising that he could afford to live in the area. But his flat was very small, tucked at the back of an old block and scarcely modernised. He had rented it since the early 1960s, having previously lived for several years in a small hotel. To reach Patrick, you walked through the outer courtyard to a second inner courtyard and climbed one flight of wooden stairs to his front door.

Inside the apartment, a narrow corridor led to the right to the bathroom and kitchen. Immediately ahead of the front door was a book-lined passage that opened into the sitting room, with the bedroom beyond. The rooms were small: the sitting room measured about 12 or 13 feet square and the bedroom was even smaller. The kitchen was large enough to eat in, with a small table in the middle and a window overlooking the courtyard. Had Katherine not seen the Duval apartment she was sure that she would quite easily have believed that all Parisian flats came with only two rooms.

Patrick had never married and his flat had a distinctly masculine air. The bookshelves were crammed with reference books of every kind but no fiction, of which Patrick disapproved. A dark-wood desk crowded with papers and an ancient typewriter and a leather swivel chair were tight up against the left-hand wall of the sitting room. An old leather sofa and two armchairs filled most of the rest of the space. The far wall was dominated by a huge surrealist painting by a friend of Patrick's called Max, which depicted a dark blue night with a strange shadowy tree and a man's face hanging in the sky. The bedroom had a rather high double bed, a wardrobe and a wooden chair. Rugs lay on the wood floors in this part of the flat. The kitchen and bathroom floors were covered in linoleum.

Katherine took to visiting Patrick quite often. The big advantage was that he had a bathroom, so typically Katherine had a bath there when she went to visit. Patrick also fed her. He was vegetarian but at first he insisted on buying Katherine meat, so long as she cooked it. As he munched on celeriac salad or gnocchi, Katherine chewed on steak. Eventually, she persuaded him that she was quite happy to eat as he did, which made life simpler for him and made her feel more comfortable.

Sometimes, they went to the local patisserie and indulged themselves with a madeleine, the shell-shaped sponge cake made famous by Proust, or a religieuse, a feather-light mix of choux pastry and cream, to eat after the cheese that was the inevitable second course. Wine and water flowed at these meals and very strong coffee finished them. Patrick had a passion for dark chocolate, 'chocolat à croquer', and always had a few pieces with his coffee. Katherine found it too bitter.

Patrick was a very vain man who had not yet come to terms

with the fact that he was no longer a young Adonis. In his twenties and thirties, he had cut a considerable dash, given that he was more than six feet tall, had thick, blond hair and the most startling blue eyes. By the time Katherine knew him, Patrick was nearly 60, still very trim but with snow-white rather than blond hair. The eyes, of course, were the same but they gave him a slightly mad, staring look, possibly because his eyelashes were very pale.

Occasionally, some of Patrick's friends were at the flat. Max was a regular visitor. He came from Hungary and spoke French with a dark, foreign accent. In his late thirties, Max sported a large moustache and wild, brown hair already streaked with grey. Patrick thought that Max could become an important figure in twentieth century painting, if only he would focus on his work. Katherine secretly thought his paintings were highly derivative and that his ego was the greatest thing about him. But he had a certain appealing wildness.

Michelle was a healer. She believed that removing static was therapeutic and the way to do this was to stroke fingers lightly across the temples from just under the eyes towards the back of the head and then shake the fingers to release bad energy. Michelle also had a little gadget that she would place in someone's ear and from which she could tell what was wrong with any part of their body. At least, that was what Patrick told Katherine, who never saw the apparatus in action.

Michelle and Max were typical of Patrick's set – younger than him, outwardly unconventional and without obvious means of financial support. Katherine did not particularly like them but they did impress her.

10

Caretaking

The concierge kept the area around her loge tidy, looked after the mail, took messages and acted the inquisitor of any strangers who came looking for friends in the block. The cleaning of the public areas – the staircases, the lifts and the courtyard – was the responsibility of a man of indeterminate age. His long, thin face was pockmarked from some childhood disease and he had a straggly moustache that drooped over his lips like a second-rate Dali imitation. His greasy brown hair was thinning on top and his body too was thin and slightly bent. Katherine saw him occasionally wielding a broom or mop. She did not care for the look of him but had no reason to talk to him so simply avoided looking him in the eye.

One morning, as she headed down the stairs from her room, she had turned the first corner when she came across him, bent over on the stair, apparently reading intently. She could not get past and asked him, politely, to move. He turned his face towards hers and grinned a toothless grin.

'Look,' he cried out enthusiastically, waving a magazine at her. 'Look, don't you find this exciting?'

He thrust the magazine at her and she had no choice but to look. The pictures showed a man with his penis erect and a woman kneeling in front of him sucking on it.

'Good, huh?'

Katherine felt a mixture of loathing and panic in equal measures. He moved just enough for her to have to squeeze past and she hurried down, his laughter pursuing her until she reached the safety of the courtyard. From that moment, she took great care to check he was not around before she ventured out.

11

Terri

Terri arrived in Paris very late indeed. The exchange programme had found a post for her at the very last moment – one more day and she would have been back at college.

Katherine had mixed feelings about Terri's arrival. They had been close during much of their first two years at college but Terri's personality was so strong that Katherine often felt that she was being propelled along by events beyond her control. Terri had an idea and Katherine was expected to fall in with it. Worse, any friends that Katherine made, more specifically any male friends, were immediately appropriated by Terri as her own. When it seemed that Terri would not get an exchange posting, Katherine had been secretly relieved. She could be her own person and sort her own life out. But now Terri was back in the picture.

Terri was everything that Katherine was not. She was the first member of her family to have gone to university – her father worked in a textiles factory and her mother was a school helper. They lived in Liverpool and the shock of Terri's red hair was dramatic tribute to the Irish blood in the family. She was as outspoken and direct as Katherine was subtle and indirect. Terri was quick-witted and sharp and had read voraciously since she was four – but she was not polished. Her taste in clothes was dubious – purple hot pants and an orange sweater were her idea of smart dress – and her accent resolutely declared, 'I am working class and proud of it.' She had expected most of her fellow students to be soft, middle-class intellectuals with about as much street sense as a poodle – and so she had found them.

But, for whatever reason, she had a soft spot for Katherine. Terri was a sponge; typically, she latched on to people and drew from them all the knowledge that she wanted and then moved on. She had stayed close to Katherine unusually long.

Most of the girls who knew Terri couldn't understand why men seemed to buzz around her like workers around the queen bee. She was not pretty in conventional terms because none of her features was of the standard proportion – her eyes were too small, her mouth too big and her nose a little too turned up. Her hair was a glorious colour but she did nothing with it; it just hung down, straight and lank to her shoulders. As is often the case with redheads, her skin was pale and highly freckled. She was neither thin nor fat and of average height. And yet, she could make any man believe that she thought him the cleverest, most interesting person she had ever met – and that is a very appealing attribute in any female.

They met at the Zoo de Vincennes because Terri was living nearby and wanted to show Katherine the flat. It was very modern and bright and belonged to a divorcee who let one of the rooms to Terri. Terri had fallen on her feet – every luxury denied to Katherine was there – bathroom, kitchen, easy chairs, television, laundry facilities – and Katherine had to repress her jealousy as she looked around the apartment.

'You are lucky, Terri. This is fantastic,' she cried.

'Yeh, it's pretty good, isn't it? And I don't even see Francine very often because she's away working so often – so I have the place to myself most of the time. How's your room?'

'Terrible. It's tiny and I haven't even got anywhere to put any food or swing the proverbial cat. Still, it's incredibly central and I can always go to Patrick's when I want a bath.'

As soon as she had spoken, Katherine wished she had bitten her tongue.

'Who's Patrick?' asked Terri brightly.

'An old friend of my father. He's been very kind and treats me to dinner whenever I go to his place.'

'Sounds good. Do you think he'd mind if I came along one time?'

Katherine wanted to say yes, he would mind, but, of course, she didn't.

Terri entranced Patrick. She admired his reference books and asked interested questions about the paranormal, one of Patrick's pet topics, and listened rapt to his tales of skulduggery at the UN and his own time there in the 1950s. She admired Max's painting and agreed that it showed touches of real genius. She moved softly around the kitchen, pouring coffee and tossing salad, asking for advice about how best to season it. She even became very enthusiastic at the prospect of turning vegetarian; she'd been thinking about doing so for a while anyway.

After two or three such visits, Patrick began inviting Terri by herself. By the end of three or four weeks, Terri had left her cosy billet in Vincennes and moved in with the newly invigorated Patrick. Katherine's special place had been taken over.

12

Art for art's sake

One of Katherine's finals papers was going to be art history. Art history at a university other than Oxford might have been expected to focus on art but the syllabus in this instance centred on the written word – the writings of Delacroix, his very lengthy diaries, and Baudelaire, his slightly less lengthy art criticism, primarily his reviews of the Salons d'Art and his milestone commentary on the impact of photography. Katherine had dutifully purchased a three-volume edition of Delacroix's diaries, bound in bright red, and a couple of editions of Baudelaire's art criticism and she had begun to work her way slowly through the first volume of the diaries. But what really interested her was the art – and she was determined to see as much as possible while she was in Paris.

Like most visitors to Paris, she started with the Louvre. This was a long time before Pei's famous Pyramid and the redevelopment of the Louvre into an all-singing, all-dancing tourist attraction and food court. It was a much lower-key if popular affair at the turn of the 1970s and Katherine joined the crowds on a Sunday afternoon, when entrance was free.

She decided to limit herself on this first visit to the major attractions and to trying to get a feel for the place. The sheer scale of the enterprise was overwhelming. Everywhere she turned, corridors and galleries stretched out towards infinity, beckoning the explorer into worlds long past. She found the Venus de Milo quite easily but then wondered what all the fuss was about. Her eye was not sufficiently educated to take in the harmony and grace of this testament to the Greek creative spirit. She was vaguely disappointed by its size and realised that she was too aware of what was missing rather than what was there. It did not move her in the slightest.

The Nike, the Winged Victory of Samothrace, was a different story. Soaring majestically at the top of a flight of stairs, its wings outstretched, straining forward and upwards to where the eye cannot see, it struck a chord in Katherine's heart and she spent a long ten minutes transfixed by its power.

If Venus had seemed small, the Mona Lisa was tiny. Presented in a room with many other pictures, she was almost lost on the walls and was partially concealed for much of the time by the incessant throng of Japanese tourists crowding round, trying to see whether her eyes really did follow them as they moved this way and that. Some tried to take photographs. Those who had failed to adjust their cameras were pounced on by eager attendants crying, 'Pas de flash! Pas de flash!' Katherine admired her serenity and the sense that she was in control of her life. Katherine felt sure that la Gioconda knew exactly what she wanted.

Much to her surprise, though, Katherine's strongest reactions were to the serried ranks of lesser-known Greek statuary. She felt unaccountably sad as she gazed at the statues, and the bits of statues, and the friezes lining the galleries. There was something intensely honourable about the wise-looking Athenas and the beautiful, young male athletes. But their beauty and simplicity reflected a world that no longer existed. She left the antiquities section with a deep sense of regret and melancholy and decided she had seen enough at the Louvre for one day.

The other art gallery close by was the Jeu de Paume, which was almost opposite Katherine's building. Here were housed some of the greatest Impressionist works, including Monet's studies of Chartres cathedral. The day that Katherine visited the gallery for the first time the sun was shining brightly and there was too much reflection on many of the pictures.

They could have hung them better, she thought to herself as she tried to manoeuvre into a position where she could see each painting properly. And yet, in spite of the excessive light, she was overwhelmed by the beauty and colour all around her, intensified by the very intimate and personal atmosphere of the Jeu de Paume itself, a perfectly formed little building. She left the display in a state of euphoria, a broad smile on her face.

13

Jean-Luc

Josette and Anne-Marie were two of the youngest teachers at the school. Josette was slim and dark-haired, Ann-Marie equally slim but with long blonde hair tied up in a ponytail. They were friendly towards Katherine at lunch and happily quizzed her about Oxford and London and the English educational system. She got on well with them and was more pleased than she could say when they invited her to a party they were holding in their flat.

It was difficult to know what to wear. Katherine surveyed her wardrobe and despaired of finding any combination of clothes that would both fit and make her feel at all attractive. In the end, she did what she always did – put on trousers and an oversized top that hid the bulges and curves of which she was so ashamed. She spent a lot of time squinting into the mirror to apply her make-up. Her eyes were, she knew, her best feature but she had not learnt the art of less is more and, so, she piled on the eyeliner and the mascara and blue eyeshadow in a desperate attempt to make them stand out. She brushed out her hair, now reaching way below her shoulders, and applied some pink lipstick. She would do.

Josette and Ann-Marie's flat was almost as tiny as Patrick's – the ubiquitous two rooms, a small kitchen and bathroom – but the young women had an eye for colour and shape and it was very bright and welcoming. Katherine noted the cream walls and modern prints, the scatter cushions and rugs, the profusion of plants. She compared these pleasant surroundings with her own room and felt a slight pang of envy. It would have been so different if she could have shared with people like these.

It was less a party than a gathering. Music was playing very softly in the background but most of the noise was generated by the conversations emanating from several small groups of people. One of these groups included Halit, Josette's boyfriend, an Albanian who was living in forced exile in France. Halit was holding forth on his favourite subject, the oppression of the Albanian people and the need for armed insurrection. Katherine listened for a while, on the edge of the group, but then drifted towards Ann-Marie who was beckoning her over to another corner of the room.

'Katherine, let me present Jean-Luc. Jean-Luc, this is Katherine who is our assistante d'anglais this year.'

'How do you do, Katherine. I hope you are enjoying Paris?'

'Oh, yes, of course,' replied Katherine a bit too quickly. 'It's so beautiful, how could anyone not enjoy it?'

'Yes, that's true. But tell me, how long have you been here?'

'Since September.'

'So you've had plenty of time to explore. Have you been anywhere especially interesting? What do you think of the Man Ray exhibition? Have you met many interesting people?'

Jean-Luc rattled out questions like a machine gun in rapid

staccato bursts. Katherine decided she rather liked the manic energy he radiated.

'Well, I haven't been to the Man Ray yet and I've been so busy teaching and finding my bearings that apart from Josette and Ann-Marie I haven't really got to know anyone.'

'That's a very sad state of affairs; we must rectify it immediately.'

Jean-Luc took Katherine by the arm and led her off to another group. The chat ranged over a hundred and one different topics, from the state of the economy to President Pompidou's ego, from linguistics, Jean-Luc's field of research, to the aftermath of the '68 revolution. For the first time since she had come to Paris, Katherine really enjoyed herself. After a diet of meaningless conversations with Jacky, increasingly awkward visits to Patrick's flat and the very limited exchanges between her and her pupils, Katherine was in the midst of a group of intelligent, well-educated adults who listened to her opinions and shared their jokes. She hadn't realised until then how much she was missing the company of like-minded individuals.

When it was time to go, before the last metro, Jean-Luc gave her his card and suggested they meet for a drink and maybe a trip to the cinema. Katherine delightedly accepted the invitation and they set a date for Monday evening.

Katherine slept well that night.

14

Daily bread

Most days, Katherine walked to school along the Rue de Rivoli, passing as she went some of the most famous landmarks in Paris – the Louvre, Palais Royal, the Hotel de Ville, the tour St Jacques.

The western end of the road, facing the Tuileries Gardens, was the smart end. The pavement was sheltered by a colonnaded canopy lined by over-priced tourist boutiques selling silk scarves and irredeemable souvenirs. WH Smith had an English bookshop with a tea-room upstairs, where Parisian matrons could partake of Earl Grey tea and English muffins or crumpets in a wood-panelled room reminiscent of the kind of establishment you might find in Harrogate. Angelina, further east along the street, was the Parisian version of a tea-shop, a rococo riot of gilt and ornate decoration, where traditionally attired waitresses served pastries and cakes to a select clientele with both the time and the money.

Most of the boutiques were far too expensive for Katherine even to consider making a purchase in them. Her salary, paid in arrears, was just sufficient to pay the rent, travel costs and food. The food budget was greatly helped by lunchtime at the lycée. The first time that Katherine had joined her fellow teachers for lunch she had been amazed by the quality and range of food made available – salads, hot main courses, cheeses and puddings, plenty of fresh bread – these were school meals quite unlike any Katherine had encountered before. Even more surprising was the fact that on the teachers' tables there were also jugs of wine, cider and water.

Katherine resolved early on that she would eat lunch at school and effectively not eat at other times. This would surely help her to lose weight. The resolution faltered when, by early evening, she felt either hungry or depressed or both and went in search of food that she could justify to herself as healthy. It was then that Katherine discovered *Familia* muesli. A heady mixture of porridge oats, dried fruits and cane sugar, *Familia* came in pleasingly large boxes. One box ought to last at least a week. The primitive cooking facilities in her bedsit precluded Katherine from indulging in any real culinary efforts but milk or fromage blanc (a creamy soft cheese) lodged just outside the dormer window could last up to two or three days.

So it was that Katherine's daily diet, when she did not visit Patrick, followed a regular pattern. On waking, she boiled up a small pan of water and had an infusion in her room. On the way to work, on the days that she had classes, she often stopped at a café on the corner facing Palais Royal. This café, long since gone in the wake of high rents and redevelopment, served the needs of an incongruously poor clientele. It consisted of just one large open space with a bar running the length of one end. There were some chairs placed around the perimeter and in the middle of the room were small, high round tables at which customers could stand.

The prices of coffee and croissants in this café were far below the norm. It's fair to say that their quality was also inferior. The clientele tended to be elderly women dressed in ill-fitting woollen coats, old men with watery eyes, young Arabs and Africans. The coffee was thick and bitter and the croissants filling.

At school, Katherine ate well – perhaps some charcuterie, a green salad, escalope de veau and a yoghurt. Typically, she drank a glass of cider and then switched to water. It was difficult to resist the bread and she gave up counting the pieces. An apple or orange helped restore the balance, or so she rationalised.

All might have been well if Katherine had rationed her food intake in the evening. But it was hard to resist the temptation of first one and then a second bowl of muesli. If she bought fromage blanc, Katherine tended to buy the largest pot in the chiller – and then ate it in one go. A cycle of resolve, hunger, greed and guilt was soon established. If the downfall was not muesli, it was fromage blanc, if not fromage blanc, it was pâté en croûte, the French version of pork pie which was sold in handy vacuum-packs of two slices.

Katherine's weight problem was long-established. Her mother liked to see her children eat – feeding them well was her way of expressing love. Unfortunately for Katherine, of the two Stewart daughters, she was the one that could least afford to eat in the quantities that mother-love dictated. This tendency to fat became apparent in Katherine's last years at school when her academic studies took up more and more of her time and regular sports activities were increasingly put on the back burner. Her mother dismissed any comments with, 'It's just puppy-fat,' and, indeed, perhaps at that stage it was and it might well have disappeared with exercise and a reduced calorie intake but it was not to be.

Although there were many opportunities to play sports at

Oxford, Katherine persuaded herself that she did not have the time, discouraged by her first and only visit to the tennis training squad. It was not that she played worse than many of the other girls there, in fact, she had played rather well – but they were all far slimmer and more athletic-looking than she was. She could not handle the thought of competing with or training with this supremely self-confident clique and took the line of least resistance by not turning up for any further sessions.

Duncan had not helped. The couple of times they had played some friendly tennis, it had become rapidly clear that he played badly – and resented being beaten. Katherine did not press him to play again and the nearest she got to exercise thereafter was a game of croquet on the college lawns.

Of course, Katherine could have starved herself thin, as did a number of her contemporaries, but it was too easy to eat. College meals were paid for in advance at the beginning of term and each student then received a book of meal tickets, with differently coloured tickets for breakfast, lunch and dinner. It was possible to recoup a small proportion of the cost at the end of term by returning unused tickets. But the cost of college meals was, inevitably, far lower than the cost of meals outside – and on Katherine's extremely limited, student income, it made financial sense to eat in college as much as possible.

Even when she lived out of college in her second year, Katherine still ate most of the time in college as the same rules about paying for them largely applied. So, for two years, Katherine had generally eaten three square meals a day, when two would probably have been more than sufficient. In addition, there had been afternoon tea.

Tea was free at college – and something of an institution. Between four and five o'clock every day, up to half the college's student population and assorted boyfriends and others gathered in the dining hall to gossip and take tea. The attraction was an endless supply of sliced brown or white bread, strawberry jam and butter. It was not a gastronomic feast by any stretch of the imagination but the lure of bread and jam was astonishingly strong to those trying to study in the library or their rooms.

All still might have been well, however, given the calories burnt off by late nights, lack of sleep and the mere fact of being on the go every day, had medical science not made its mark. Katherine took the decision to go on the Pill after she and Duncan had begun to sleep together.

At first, they had used a condom. Neither was experienced and it had taken them a while to get used to slipping on the rubber at just the right moment. Not that Katherine participated in this part of the proceedings. She just watched as Duncan turned away and reached into the bedside drawer, pulled out a packet, unwrapped the flat, soft disc and hunching forward gently stretched it over his member. Katherine was pleased that Duncan was being so responsible but she knew that he found the procedure frustrating. They both did, if she was honest with herself. They both wanted to make love properly, without any barriers.

Although the pill had been available for several years, the jury was still out on whether there would be adverse long-term effects from interfering with the body's natural chemical processes. Many older women were reluctant to change their birth-control habits and, so, Katherine's generation was probably the first to start taking the pill in significant numbers. These second-wave participants in the sexual revolution included her best friend at college, Jane.

Jane and Katherine had hit it off from the very first day and were soon sharing midnight cups of coffee and secrets. Jane it was who told Katherine that she went for contraceptive advice at the

Brook Advisory Clinic. She offered to book Katherine in for an appointment.

A couple of weeks later, Katherine looked nervously around the waiting room. Four or five other young women were waiting their turn, flicking through magazines or reading a newspaper. The receptionist had given Katherine a form to fill out – the usual sort of thing, name, age, address, reason for visit. Katherine sat in a chair and filled the form out. She hesitated at one of the questions, 'Do you or any direct relatives suffer from any circulatory problems – history of heart attack, angina, varicose veins, other?' After some consideration, she wrote in the space provided, 'Father – two or three heart attacks/strokes.' She was never quite sure which type of attack Henry had suffered, though she knew they went back to before she was born. She did not mention that she had noticed a couple of bulging veins in her right calf, nor that she could not sit cross-legged for more than ten minutes before her legs went quite dead. Afraid that the clinic might turn her down for the pill, she decided that neither fact was important.

The examination by the doctor was cursory – weight, blood pressure, a few more questions about her medical history, which had been singularly uneventful, and a brief resume of the different types of contraception available. Katherine had known before she went that she was only interested in the pill. Alternative barrier methods seemed too messy and mechanical, no better than the condoms they were using. Spontaneity and prevention were the issues here – nothing else mattered.

One hour after entering the clinic, Katherine emerged with three months supply of tiny pills, one sheet per month, each pill encased in its own little foil pouch with a day of the week printed underneath. She was a liberated woman.

For the next year and a half, Katherine dutifully attended the clinic and renewed her subscription to the Pill generation. Weight gain was noted by the doctor but no further comments were made. Katherine was one of the unlucky ones whose body reacted to the pill by gaining weight. She gained nearly 14lb in the first year.

The doctor may have made no comments but her family was different. Both parents were shocked by the amount of weight Katherine had put on when she came home for holidays and even Penny conceded that something needed to be done. Her solution was to cut back on puddings at mealtimes and to make encouraging noises about those aspects of Katherine's appearance that could be praised – her hair, her eyes, her ankles. Penny felt sure that Katherine was putting on weight because she must be unhappy at college but she could not get anything out of her daughter, who simply said that everything was just fine.

Henry decided that shock tactics were the only solution. Unwilling to speak to her directly, he wrote Katherine a very brief note that arrived a day after Katherine's return to Oxford for Trinity term. 'My darling Katie, We are terribly concerned about your weight. The sight of you this holiday shocked your mother so much – I have not seen her so upset since the death of Grandma. Please try and do something about it. All my love Papa.'

Henry's tactics backfired. Katherine could not bring herself to phone home for several weeks.

When Katherine arrived in Paris, she had nearly five months supply of the pill. This would take her to the end of January. When the pills ran out, she could not face trying to find out how to obtain them in France. She hadn't even registered with a doctor. She decided to stop taking them. She would avoid sex and maybe lose some of the weight the pill had induced her to put on. Her New Year's Resolution, you might say.

15

Feeding the soul

Katherine had about ten hours teaching per week. Allowing for a couple of hours preparation and another couple devoted to helping out the English department in other ways, such as the recordings for the language lab, there were many hours left in the week for Katherine to pursue her own interests.

She enrolled at the Sorbonne for its *Cours de la langue et de la littérature française*. There was homework for the course, a language class and a morning of lectures. The lectures began at eight o'clock and lasted three hours. They were held in an over-heated, circular lecture theatre that reminded Katherine vaguely of the Sheldonian and, at first, she had found the contrast between young students and ancient tradition reassuringly familiar. But she found the early start increasingly daunting – and the exceptionally formal tone of the teaching methods very off-putting. The lecturers spoke for the whole of the three hours. There were no questions permitted, no dialogue. Students were expected to keep quiet, listen and take notes.

There were about 20 students in the language class. This meant that one-on-one attention was extremely limited. The exercises were dull and repetitive and made Katherine feel like she was in the first year at secondary school rather than a third-year undergraduate. She stuck the course until the Christmas break but decided she would not return in January. She had tried formal courses for the last time.

She could not spend all her time in art galleries, so she walked a good deal. Walking had the advantage, moreover, of being free. Paris, unlike London or New York, lends itself to exploration on foot and Katherine came to know 'her' city very well. She particularly liked to walk through the Tuileries Gardens and along the river, crossing over at the Pont Neuf and into the Left Bank. She explored the tiny winding streets on the Ile de la Cité and Ile St Louis, imagining how Paris must have been in the times before Haussmann instituted his grand design. She walked up the Boul' Mich and the Boulevard St Germain, window shopping and, occasionally, allowing herself the luxury of a coffee and tartine in one of the famous cafes.

Generally, Katherine enjoyed her daytime promenades, even if they had no real objective. Sometimes, she woke early and explored the local neighbourhood. In many ways, Paris was at its best in the early morning light, before the traffic had built up and the people thronged the pavements. The death warrant for Les Halles, the Covent Garden of Paris, had been signed and the market was in its last throes before being demolished. Katherine took her primitive camera with her on early morning explorations through the narrow streets and alleyways, threading her way past the huge shuttered halls that had until recently resounded with the clatter and energy of fruit and vegetable sellers and buyers.

She tried to capture the emptiness and the silence, the dark shadows and strange silver light that cast a pearly gloom along the high-sided streets. Walking through Les Halles, Katherine could almost feel time stop. She could feel the essence of what she wanted to capture – but the resulting snaps, in tiny format, fell far short of anything so poetic.

Spare time during the day could, then, bring great pleasure. The nights were different. Once school had finished or the galleries had closed, Katherine had very little option but to return to her room. She forced herself to read some of her set books and she wrote many letters but time passed very slowly inside those four pink walls. The best times were when she received letters, which she read over and over. Most precious were the letters from Peter.

Katherine had first written to Peter on a whim but with small hope that he would reply. He had been a close friend of Duncan at college but, when Duncan finished with her, Peter had been particularly kind. She had written him a chatty letter, deliberately staying off the subject of Duncan, and inviting him to write back when he could. Peter had replied within the week.

The delight at receiving this first letter turned rapidly to despair as Katherine read what Peter had to say about Duncan. Peter wrote that he felt he had to put the record straight about Duncan because he had been so unfair to Katherine. He hoped that she would not mind too terribly if he told her that Duncan had been two-timing her during the last term with a girl called Susanna. He felt that Duncan had led Katherine along and hadn't been totally honest about why he had finished with her. He hoped this wasn't too much of a shock – and promised to write again soon.

Katherine flung herself down on the bed and wept. Wave upon wave of choking sobs shook her body. She cried until she could cry no more. She did not know how long she lay on her bed. She became aware that it was dark outside and turned on her light. She felt cold and empty. Not only had Duncan rejected her – he had cheated on her. She felt stupid for having cared so much about him and stupid for having been so blind. She decided she would not think about him again.

Some days later, Katherine wrote back to Peter, calmly and cheerfully, filling her letter with amusing details of daily life at the lycée and what she hoped were illuminating descriptions of the Paris cityscape. She thanked him for telling her about Duncan and suggested they not talk about him further. Peter replied promptly and so began a regular correspondence that became for Katherine something of a lifeline. He wrote wittily about his fellow students on the teacher training course he had enrolled in and touchingly about his family in Belfast. His younger brother was still at school and his widowed mother had no option but to stay there. Peter felt guilty that he was safe in Nottingham when his family were experiencing all the fears and real dangers of an Ulster torn apart by violence. Katherine was a sympathetic correspondent.

16

Paris by night

But letters could occupy only a relatively small part of Katherine's free time. Often back at her room by four in the afternoon, she found herself increasingly anxious to get out of the room by early evening. Rather than face the blank walls, she found excuses to go shopping – or at least window-shopping. There was a department store close by, the Grands Magasins du Louvre, long since gone, and Katherine made regular pilgrimages to its food hall and stationery departments. It was there that she discovered muesli.

Sometimes, she bought herself a new biro or walked through the perfumery section, inhaling the exotic scents as they wafted through the air and admiring the elegant bottles ranged behind the shiny glass counters. She did not dare to try any of the scents from the demonstration bottles – she knew she could not possibly afford to buy any and would find it embarrassing if approached by one of the exquisitely made-up young women in their white coats.

Not all such expeditions turned out well. Katherine had noticed advertisements for what she took to be a department store on the north side of the city and which appeared to have unusually late opening hours. So, one evening, she decided to visit it. The nearest metro station to Galéries Barbès was Barbès Rochechouart, a journey of around half-an-hour by metro.

It had briefly crossed Katherine's mind that the location seemed a bit unlikely for a major department store but the advertisements had been quite clear. The lack of many other passengers in the train struck her as a bit strange but she stuck her nose into her book and soon she was at her destination. Coming out into the night, Katherine was surprised at how dismal this part of Paris was, quite unlike the well-lit bustle of the Rue de Rivoli or the urgent comings and goings around the two major central stores, Au Printemps and Galéries Lafayette. Then turning towards the store, she could read the name in large letters on the building, she realised her mistake. Galéries Barbès was a furniture store. She did not even go in, there would have been no point. She returned to her room, defeated by the pointlessness of the journey.

A short walk from the Rue de Rivoli stands the Opéra de Paris. Its baroque mass dominates the junction of several major boulevards laid out by Baron Haussmann in his re-design of Paris in the nineteenth century. Around the corner from this monument to French culture was the Drugstore de l'Opéra, which you could say was a monument to American culture. It was open until late into the night and offered the insomniac shopper everything from clothing to books and music, or even aspirin. Brightly lit, noisy and ultra-modern, the drugstore was an irresistible magnet for Katherine when she felt the compulsion to go out in the evenings. She could not have explained to herself, let alone anyone else, why she went to the drugstore. She had virtually no money, and, so, she never bought anything there. Rather, she moved through the store quite quickly, glancing at the odd book, thinking about buying a magazine and then changing her mind, idly sifting through clothes on a rail. Once she tried on a pair of corduroy trousers but was horrified to find that they did not fit, despite their being ostensibly a size larger than her existing clothes. Perhaps it was comforting to know that there were other aimless souls – the drugstore had its fair share of observers rather than participants – at a loose end in the city.

During one of these empty excursions, a man came up to her as she was flicking through Paris Match.

'Mademoiselle,' he spoke softly into her ear. 'Have you ever thought about modelling?'

Katherine turned round and stared hard at the man.

'What on earth are you talking about? Please go away.'

'But Mademoiselle, you have such a wonderful shape. I run a studio. I know men who would pay good money to photograph you. Look, don't worry; it's quite legitimate. Bring your father, bring your boyfriend – you're not married are you? Bring your husband. It is all very tasteful – and you would not see the men yourself. It would be quite safe.'

'Don't be ridiculous.'

'Look, here is my card. Telephone me if you change your mind. You could earn 500 francs for a session – minimum.'

The strange man disappeared, leaving Katherine holding his business card, 'Guy Fortrain, Photographe'. 500 francs a session, that was half a month's salary. Katherine did not know whether to be shocked or amused. Either way, she was not that desperate.

17

Jean-Luc two

Jean-Luc was doing research into linguistics while working for International House. He was 30 and had spent the whole of his adult life in academic study. Slight of build, sandy-haired and sporting John Lennon glasses, he looked the part. Katherine came to view her nights out, or in, with Jean-Luc as some kind of salvation.

They hosted small supper parties for Jean-Luc's friends who stayed late into the night, dipping into salad, drinking wine and arguing about whether the '68 revolution had meant anything - and they went to the cinema to watch ancient Hollywood movies. Paris was home to an enthusiastic audience of cinéphiles who happily queued at rundown art cinemas to watch re-releases of the likes of Casablanca and White Heat. Katherine adored the cinema of the 1930s and 1940s and she and Jean-Luc played games to see who could identify some obscure bit-part player first. Jean-Luc tended to favour the gangster movies and the films noirs. Katherine agreed about the films noirs but was less keen on the gangsters. Both agreed that It's a Wonderful Life and Citizen Kane were almost beyond criticism.

It seemed to Katherine that at last she had found someone with whom she could have a civilised relationship. Jean-Luc never came to her lodgings, she always went to his apartment, which was little more than a studio with small kitchen and bathroom attached. There were piles of books and newspapers, a desk overflowing with Jean-Luc's latest research, a wardrobe full of his clothes (he was something of a dandy) and a huge bed. They spent many happy hours in the bed. Jean-Luc was attentive and Katherine responsive.

Jean-Luc took Katherine to the Man Ray exhibition. It was the first major retrospective of the famed photographer and surrealist for many years and nearly all his most famous pieces were on show, including the iron with nails driven through it and the photograph of a woman's face weeping glass tears. Jean-Luc loved it. He declared that Man Ray embodied the very soul of art, or some such, whereas Katherine disliked almost everything she saw.

'I agree he's very clever,' she said as they walked out of the exhibition, 'but he's so cold. I don't find any emotion in anything he does – it's all surface. And a lot of his stuff just seems pretentious. I just don't get it.'

'Perhaps that's because you're too young to appreciate his philosophy of life,' countered Jean-Luc. He said it in a half-joking way but Katherine noted that this was the first time that Jean-Luc had even mentioned the difference in their ages.

In her eagerness for the relationship to work, Katherine had failed to notice the tell-tale signs that perhaps Jean-Luc was less committed than she was. He cancelled a couple of dates at short notice. He went off to talk to other young women in the middle of parties. He suggested gently to her that perhaps she didn't want pudding or cheese at the end of a meal. He began to find reasons why she should go home rather than stay the night.

Jean-Luc was torn. He enjoyed Katherine's company. She was clever and interested in many of the same things that he enjoyed. Her personality was engaging and she had a good sense of humour. But, she was too obvious about her desire for some greater commitment than he was willing to give. And she was not slim or chic or gamine. She was frankly rather dumpy. They didn't look good together.

On their last evening he took her to see Key Largo. They queued happily in the rain before the doors opened – and then spent a magical hour and a half in the company of Bogart, Bacall and Edward G Robinson. Jean-Luc accompanied Katherine to the metro where he told her in two sentences that it was all over.

'Katherine, as you know I do not love you. I don't think we should see each other again.'

As you know – *comme tu t'en doutes* – the phrase echoed over and over in Katherine's brain. No, she hadn't known. She hadn't doubted anything.

Jean-Luc disappeared to the opposite platform to wait for his train, which arrived before hers. He did not look back or across at her. He simply vanished. Katherine's journey home was a blur.

18

Happy families

Not long after the break-up with Jean-Luc, as Katherine was leaving school to make her way home, Josiane, one of the particularly friendly girls in deuxième ran to catch her up.

'Katherine, please wait,' she called after her. 'My mother was wondering if you would like to come and spend Friday night with us so you could celebrate the Sabbath with us.'

'That's very kind but I'm not Jewish, you know.'

'Yes, I know, but that doesn't matter. We thought you might find it interesting and it would be so nice to share it with you.'

Katherine stood quite still, surprised and touched by the invitation.

'I should love to. Please thank your mother.'

Friday afternoon came and Katherine made her way to the Bernstein apartment, just around the corner from Arts et Métiers metro station. Madame Bernstein and her three daughters, Naomi, Josiane and Lily, greeted Katherine warmly as they ushered her into the living room. Here, for the first time since her arrival in Paris, Katherine found herself in a real family home. On the walls there were family photographs, pictures drawn or painted by the girls and a couple of bright watercolours. At the sitting end of the room, the two sofas were strewn with a patchwork of cushions and in the corner of one snoozed a large tabby cat. An old but highly polished table surrounded by six high-backed dining chairs filled the other end of the room.

'Come on in, Katherine,' said Madame Bernstein. 'I'm so pleased to meet you. Josiane enjoys your classes so much – it's a long time since I've heard her be so enthusiastic about school.'

'That's very kind of you, Madame. I enjoy teaching Josiane and her class. They make it very easy for me, you know.'

'Good, good,' beamed Madame. 'Josiane tells me you haven't celebrated the Sabbath before, so I do hope the evening won't disappoint. Will you help lay the table?'

The girls busied themselves fetching cutlery and plates and napkins from a large sideboard while Madame directed Katherine to the wine and water glasses. By the time they had finished, the table looked very inviting – shining glassware, creamy damask napkins, silver candlesticks.

The door to the apartment opened and in came Monsieur Bernstein. He kissed his wife, shook Katherine's hand and disappeared briefly to wash and brush up. Then the evening's celebration began.

Madame said a brief prayer over the candles as she lit them and then Monsieur blessed the bread and wine. The meal was simple but delicious – chollah bread followed by grilled fish, potatoes and green beans; a large salad; fresh fruit, dates and nuts, black coffee. The conversation was lively, with all the girls chipping in and interrupting each other with jokes and stories. Katherine was surprised at how much fun it all was; she had had no idea what to expect.

The family insisted that Katherine stay the night - a bed was ready for her in the bedroom occupied by the two younger girls.

'Do you mind turning off the light, Katherine?' asked Josiane as they were turning in. 'Then we won't be breaking the Sabbath by working. It seems silly but in theory we shouldn't be turning power on and off.'

'What do you normally do?'

'Maman does it – but, as you are here, tomorrow morning would you also mind putting on the coffee in the kitchen?'

'No, of course not, I should be pleased to do so.'

Katherine turned off the light and felt her way back to her bed. As she lay there in the darkness, she felt more positive and happier than she had since coming to Paris. The meal had been a wonderful occasion and Katherine felt quite privileged to have been invited to share in it.

After returning to her room on Saturday, Katherine went to the local café and phoned home. She chatted enthusiastically about her trips to art galleries and the old films she had been to see. And about her stay with the Bernsteins.

'Mummy, you'd really like them,' she told Penny. 'They're so kind and friendly. It was so good to be with a normal family for a bit. Almost like being at home.'

'That's wonderful, darling. I'm glad you're sounding so happy. Do you think you're beginning to settle in properly now?'

'Absolutely. I really feel as though I'm beginning to understand how to get the best out of being here – and my French is improving every day. Most of the girls are really nice and Patrick has been very kind. I miss everyone at home but it won't be long before I'm back for Christmas and I'll be able to fill you in much better then.'

'Splendid. I'm looking forward to it. We miss you too, you know.'

19

Happy birthday

Katherine woke on her birthday to the sound of driving rain beating against the dormer window. She dressed quickly and ran down the stairs to see if she had any post. The concierge handed her three envelopes and Katherine rushed back to her room. There were birthday cards from home (one from each of her parents) and a letter from Peter. She put the cards up on her desk to join the ones sent by Emily and Jane, which had arrived earlier in the week, and tore open Peter's letter. It was quite coincidental that it had arrived on her birthday.

His letter was the usual mix of anecdotes about student life and reflections on his family. But on the last page Peter mentioned that he had met a girl called Louise at a party and that they had hit it off straightaway. They had been going out together now for three weeks. Katherine put the letter down and listened to the rain. Of course, she and Peter were, in that well-worn phrase, just good friends but Katherine had enough self-awareness to realise that she had been secretly hoping that when she returned home at the end of the year they might have met up and meant more to each other. Peter had written his words carefully: he recognised how much store Katherine put on their correspondence and he did not want to hurt her. But, equally, he had only feelings of kind friendship towards her, nothing more – and he had decided that he needed to put some distance between them. Meeting Louise had given him the opportunity.

Katherine took a deep breath and folded the letter back into its envelope before placing it in the box where she kept all Peter's letters. She opened the window and, standing on a chair, craned her neck around the opening to look at the Eiffel Tower. Its dark familiar silhouette stood out against a sky that was purple-black with rainclouds and some spots of rain hit her face. She was glad of the cooling effect on her hot cheeks and, after some minutes, she climbed down from the chair.

Drying off her face with a towel, Katherine decided that she had to go out – after all, it was her birthday so she should go out and enjoy it. She pulled on her raincoat, grabbed one of the books she was currently reading from her bedside and put it in her bag, and locked the door behind her.

Having made her way downstairs, she hesitated at the huge street door because she had no idea where she was going. She pressed the release button and the door clicked open. As she stepped out into the street she turned left and started to walk up the Rue de Rivoli. She realised she was on automatic pilot by the time she reached the corner of the block. This was the way she went to school.

Having committed herself, she carried on up the road, slightly hunched forward in the face of the rain. The weather had deterred most people from venturing out so she had the pavement largely to herself and made rapid progress. Having walked most of the length of the road, Katherine realised that her raincoat and legs were both soaked. She decided to have a drink and dry off in a café. So, she toasted her birthday with a milky coffee.

By the time that Katherine had finished her drink and read a couple of chapters of *The Godfather*, the rain had eased off and only a few desultory drops were still falling. She decided to cross the river in her by now established pattern but, today, she would visit the Sainte Chapelle before crossing into the Left Bank.

The Sainte Chapelle stands around the corner from its more famous cousin Notre Dame cathedral. Almost hidden behind the Prefecture de Police, the chapel rises tall, slender and mysterious, hiding its beauty from the casual observer. Once inside, however, the spectator soon realises why this building is among Paris's most treasured jewels. A simple church on two levels, the chapel is graced on its upper level, that reserved in earlier times for the king and his entourage, by magnificent stained glass windows that throw shafts of magical colour from the length and height of its stone walls.

Katherine had not visited the Sainte Chapelle before but she had read about it. So, her visit was less a journey of discovery than it might have been for someone coming to it in complete ignorance. And, yet, she had the greatest luck in visiting it at a time when there was no-one else inside and, just as she stepped into the dark, slightly musty atmosphere that characterises almost any church more than 100 years old, the sun came out from behind the thinning clouds.

An explosion of colour filled the space. Dust particles danced in the reds and blues and greens falling across the empty space and Katherine lost herself momentarily in the beauty that had been revealed to her. For a few, precious minutes she forgot about cramped rooms and cold showers and disappointing relationships. Then, the click-clack of heels coming into the chapel brought her back to reality.

As she came out of the Sainte Chapelle, Katherine's eyes watered in the sudden daylight and she could feel the salty sting of tears beginning to well up. She stopped and took several deep breaths to compose herself before setting off towards the bridge. By the time she had crossed over the river, she was calm but strangely deflated. She stared up the boulevard, trying to decide what she was going to do now. She walked slowly past the bookshops, pausing to rummage in the boxes of marked-down books set out on tables on the pavement. Nothing caught her eye and she continued her aimless journey.

Crossing over the Boul' Mich to the other side, the side that leads to the Sorbonne, she stopped in front of a shoe shop. The window was dressed elegantly with just eight pairs of shoes displayed. They included a pair of black patent stiletto-heeled court shoes and some very strappy sandals but the shoes that caught Katherine's attention were a pair of bright red, leather mules.

Katherine liked shoes. She had neat feet and shoes were one of the few items of clothing that she did not feel embarrassed to try on; there was never any problem about whether they would fit. She went inside and an assistant came forward almost immediately.

'Good morning, Mademoiselle. May I show you anything?'

'Good morning. Yes. I should like to see the red shoes you have in the window.'

'Ah, of course, they're very fashionable,' replied the assistant. 'What size?'

'38, I think.'

The girl went off to the store-room and Katherine sat down

on one of the plush-covered seats. She realised that the mules were completely impractical and that she couldn't really afford to buy them. But, they were so bright and modern – and it was her birthday.

The mules fitted, hardly surprising as they had no back, and they had unusually high heels, lifting Katherine up by two inches. She looked down at her feet and then in the mirror. Her ankles looked very slim and the leather shone brightly. She would take them.

'How much are they?' she asked, as she turned this way and that admiring their effect.

'Only 79 francs, mademoiselle,' replied the girl.

Only 79 francs. That was half a week's disposable income. More relevantly, it would leave her with just 43 francs for the next week and a half before she was paid. It was an absurd idea. But she did like the shoes – and sometimes being rational is not the answer. Katherine bought the mules and decided to wear them straightaway. The shop-girl put her old shoes into a box and Katherine left the shop happily teetering on her brand-new feet.

It took a little while to get used to walking in the mules – and Katherine's progress was further hampered by her efforts to avoid the remaining puddles on the pavement. She managed to walk back as far as the Place Notre Dame but her feet were aching and her legs were beginning to feel tired. So, she blew a proportion of her remaining funds on a lemonade at a nearby café, where she changed out of the mules and back into her more workaday bar-shoes.

Once she had climbed the stairs to her room, she realised that she was feeling very hungry. She filled a bowl with muesli and added the last of a carton of milk. The food tasted good and she relaxed onto her bed. Stretching out she picked up the bag and took her new mules out of the box to admire them. Turning them over, she noticed a small nick in the left heel. It was a very small nick and no-one else would even notice it was there. But she knew.

20

Patrick and Terri

Katherine phoned Patrick to see how he was and find out when she could visit him to take a bath.

'Katherine, how delightful to hear from you. Look, we're going to the Man Ray tomorrow. Why don't you join us and come back with us to the flat in the evening. It'll be lovely to see you.'

Now, Katherine had not told Patrick or Terri about Jean-Luc and she did not want to go into explanations over the phone. So, instead of saying that she had in fact already been to the exhibition, she accepted the invitation.

Once she had hung up, she wished she had had the courage to say no for once in her life.

Katherine found that her second trip to the exhibition merely served to confirm her first impressions and she was pleased to find that Patrick also had reservations about the greatness of Man Ray's art.

'Of course, the French think he's wonderful,' said Patrick. 'He appeals to their intellectual snobbery because he's an American who lives in France and believes that only the French really understand him. So, they've adopted him as one of their own. And, because he has chosen France, he's clearly a superior being.'

Katherine reflected that the same could in a small way be said of Patrick himself but refrained from making any such comment.

The evening went well. While Katherine was taking her bath, Max and his girlfriend Jocelyne arrived. Jocelyne was only a few years younger but a good deal more glamorous than Katherine's mother. She was the kind of woman who would never allow herself to be seen in public before she had applied her makeup. Her careful coiffure, expensive skirt and blouse and perfectly manicured hands were in sharp contrast to Max's habitually tousled look and studied air of artiste manqué. But Jocelyne liked to collect creative types, whom she could finance and in whose reflected glory she could bask as a patron of the arts. Since her divorce some ten years previously, she had had three main protégés of whom Max was the latest and, indeed, the longest lasting.

Patrick pressed a chilled white wine into Katherine's hand after she had emerged from her bath and Terri squeezed along the sofa to make space for her. The conversation batted back and forth and Katherine found she was enjoying it in spite of herself. Jocelyne was charming and even Max managed to talk to her without giving the impression that he would rather be somewhere else. Terri suggested to Katherine that they go into the kitchen and finalise the preparations for supper and Katherine complied.

'So, what are you up to nowadays? We haven't seen you for ages.'

Katherine noted the 'we'.

'Oh, nothing much – school, the odd cinema trip.' She still resisted the opportunity to say anything about Jean-Pierre.

'Well, it's just great you could come today. We should do this more often – there are loads of exhibitions we could go and see.'

There was that 'we' again. Katherine felt impelled to ask.

'So, are you and Patrick serious, then?'

'I'm not sure what you mean,' Terri replied carefully. 'He is the most fascinating man I've ever met and we're getting along really well. But, of course, it can't last forever. I mean, there's college next year – and who knows what will happen in the future. But, at the moment, it's just great and I can't see any reason why it shouldn't carry on while I'm here.'

'But what does Patrick think is going to happen?'

'Oh, I'm sure he knows the score. He's been around a lot longer than either of us, after all.'

Yes, that was true. Patrick was technically old enough to be Terri's grandfather, let alone father. How could Terri bring herself to have sex with him? Perhaps she closed her eyes.

'Could you get out the oil and vinegar?' Terri asked, changing the subject. 'We're going to have pasta and salad, just for a change!'

The meal was ready and everyone trooped gaily into the kitchen. The pasta, spinach-filled ravioli with a spicy tomato sauce, was declared a great success and the red wine flowed along with the conversation. Much of the gossip meant nothing to Katherine but the stories told by the assembled guests were amusingly bitchy even to an outsider.

The chatter turned to the imminent Christmas break.

'We have decided to take to the Alps,' Jocelyne declared. 'I really must get away from all the traffic and noise here – and it will be so good for Max to re-charge his artistic batteries among the pine trees and snow.'

Max shifted in his chair as though in recognition both of his own lack of say in where they were going and possibly some embarrassment at Jocelyne's rather high-flown manner.

'Well, we are going to Beirut,' countered Patrick, smiling fondly at Terri across the table. 'It's such an elegant city, Terri really should get to see it and there is the added benefit that we can get away from all the false Christmas nonsense. France used to be so much more civilised but I fear the commercialisation of religious festivals is inexorably taking over.'

Terri decided to interrupt Patrick before he could get fully into his stride. 'Yes, I'm really excited about going to Beirut. I haven't been further east than Italy.'

Katherine turned towards Terri, 'But what about your family? Won't they be expecting to see you?'

'Oh, they don't mind. We never do much at Christmas anyway.'

Katherine could not imagine what her family would say if she decided to swan off somewhere else instead of spending Christmas at home. Christmas had always been important in the Stewart household; it was the one time of the year when rituals and customs were closely observed simply because they had always been observed and nobody dared question their existence. So, there were Christmas stockings, attendance at church, turkey or goose for the Christmas dinner, toasting the Queen after her television broadcast and playing charades in the evening.

For some years Katherine had thought that Christmas was something of a con trick, all shiny lights but no real substance. Going to church seemed a particularly hypocritical activity, given that no-one in the family attended church at any other time of the year, and, yet, it was reassuringly familiar to sing carols and listen to the vicar sermonising about love and goodwill.

'Neither do we but there's no way I couldn't go home for it.'

'Ah, my dear,' said Patrick in a mock-grave voice, 'you will know you are truly an adult when you can choose not to go home for Christmas.'

Katherine flushed at the jibe but could think of nothing suitably clever to counter it.

21

Mother love

Late in the afternoon of 27 December, Penny Stewart went to take an early bath. Her head had started to ache shortly after lunch and she had taken a couple of codeine in the hope of knocking the pain quickly out of her system – but the headache had persisted and she decided that a long, warm soak in the bath would do the trick instead.

Everyone else in the house was busy with their own activities and didn't notice time passing. Katherine was writing a letter and Emily was in the kitchen preparing supper. Henry was in the study working on his latest short story. He had mixed himself a particularly fine gin and tonic, a little early but then it was Christmas, and was busily typing what he hoped would be a winning romantic fantasy to be snapped up by the women's magazines.

Nearly two hours after Penny had gone upstairs, someone said, 'Where's Penny?' Afterwards, Katherine could not remember if it had been her father or Emily who asked.

'She went upstairs for a bath.'

'That was a long time ago. Pop up and see if she's alright,' Katherine. And ask her if she'd like a drink.'

Katherine went upstairs, telling herself to remember to post her letter when she came back down. She knocked on the bathroom door, no reply.

'Mummy, you ok?'

No reply.

Katherine turned the bathroom handle and opened the door. There, slumped in the bath, was her mother, her head to one side and her frightened eyes staring out at Katherine.

'Mummy, what happened? Can you speak?'

Penny grunted incomprehensibly. Katherine turned quickly out of the room and raced down the stairs. She grabbed hold of Emily.

'Come quick. Mummy's collapsed.'

The two daughters raced back upstairs and together managed to haul their mother out of the bath and, after much effort, lifted her onto her bed. They dried her as thoroughly as they could and pulled a nightdress over her limp form.

Emily reached for the phone and called the doctor. Luckily it was late evening surgery and she was able to speak to him directly.

'Keep her warm and I'll come over as soon as I've finished here,' he instructed Emily. Meanwhile, Katherine had gone downstairs and told Henry as best she could what had happened. Henry rushed out of the room and up the stairs to his beloved Penelope. She lay propped up in bed, her eyes staring ahead, one arm lying awkwardly outside the sheet.

'Darling, darling. What's the matter?'

Penny tried to form her mouth into words but nothing came out. Henry sat next to her on the bed and took her hand.

'You're going to be fine, darling, absolutely fine.'

He was still there when the doctor arrived.

After examining Penny and asking Katherine and Emily what had happened, Dr Richards concluded that Penny must have suffered from a stroke. Her right arm and side appeared to be paralysed and her mouth was drooping slightly. A hopeful sign was that she was already beginning to recover some speaking capability, though only with immense effort

'It's really not as bad as it seems,' he reassured the family. 'There is every possibility that Penelope will recover, given time and care. She'll need help from all of you but she's a strong-willed woman and if anyone can pull through a stroke, she can.

'We need to send her to hospital straightaway. With strokes, there's always the possibility of a second episode happening relatively soon afterwards – so she needs to be kept under observation. Could I borrow the phone?'

'Well, I'd better go and pack her a bag,' said Emily. 'Why don't you make some tea or coffee or something, Katherine?'

Emily had moved into efficient, elder sister mode. Katherine busied herself with the kettle. Dr Richards returned to say that he had arranged for an ambulance, which would arrive within the hour.

The ambulance men lifted Penny out of bed and put her onto a stretcher, which they then carried carefully down the stairs and into the ambulance. Penny had revived enough to wave her functioning hand rather grandly at everybody as she passed and someone joked that it must be the Queen. Henry and Emily went with the ambulance to the hospital, leaving behind a subdued Katherine.

Father and daughter returned three hours later and reported that Penny was comfortable. No-one slept well that night.

At 12.30pm on 28 December, the Stewart family was sitting in a small office off the ward, waiting for the consultant.

The consultant came in and sat down.

''Mr Stewart, has your wife suffered recently from any unusual symptoms?'

'Well, she's been suffering from migraines for a while but I can't think of anything else.'

'Hold on, Daddy,' Katherine interrupted. 'What about when she felt odd in Selfridges?'

'When was this?' asked the doctor.

'In the summer. She and I went into town to look for clothes for me and a birthday present for one of our cousins, Fred I think. Anyway, we were in Selfridges cafe when suddenly she felt really strange and wobbly. She said she couldn't breathe properly and was going all hot and cold and feeling sick. She looked really awful – and I asked if there was a store nurse. We went up to the offices and a nurse had a look at her and let her lie down in a dark room. We stayed there for maybe 40 minutes. Mummy felt better by then and we took a taxi home. She was much better by the time we got home and she insisted that it must have been something she ate.'

'Did she go to see her doctor?'

'No, she doesn't like doctors.' Katherine wished instantly that she hadn't said that.

'Pity, we might have caught it earlier.'

'Caught what?' said Henry anxiously.

'Well,' replied the consultant very carefully. 'I'm reasonably convinced that your wife has not had a stroke. We are not certain but we believe that she may have a tumour.'

No-one spoke. A tumour. Cancer. Why couldn't it be a stroke – people recovered from strokes with enough physiotherapy and enough love. Look at Mrs Robinson three doors away. Strokes were nothing – but a tumour.

'Look, we think that we should send Mrs Stewart to Atkinson Morley's Hospital. They have developed a revolutionary method of brain scanning that should help us confirm whether or not there's a tumour. The first scan they carried out just three months ago revealed a frontal lobe tumour, which the surgeon was then able to operate on. I've already asked whether they'd be willing to look at your wife, if you agree. If the scan confirms that it is a tumour, we'll then need to find out what can be done, depending on how advanced it is.'

'Of course, of course,' Henry replied automatically. 'When?'

'Tomorrow. They don't have a bed available today.'

Henry went to see Penny and held her hand and made reassuring noises about how much better she would be soon. He did not mention the consultant's diagnosis and Penny didn't ask.

The results came through late the following afternoon. The neurologist asked Henry alone in to his office but he insisted that Emily and Katherine accompany him.

'Mr Stewart, I am sorry to say the news is not good. Your wife has an inoperable tumour on the left side of her brain. There really is nothing we can do for her here.'

Henry sank into his chair. It was inconceivable that his young, his beautiful Penny could be about to die. He was the weak one, she was the strong one. She was not meant to die before him.

'Is there nothing you can do?' he asked.

'Realistically, very little. We can give her drugs to control any pain and keep down some of the swelling – but, ultimately, I'm afraid her condition is too far advanced for anything other than palliative care.'

'How long has she got?' asked Emily.

'Well, it's always difficult to predict with any accuracy how any cancer will develop.'

'But?' interrupted Katherine.

'Well, it could be weeks or, at best, a couple of months.'

The father and his two daughters sat in shocked silence. Penny was only 47 years old. She had always been the steady one, the beautiful wife, the loving mother, the heart of the family. How could she die, now?

Henry and the doctor went to tell Penny. It was not at all clear that she fully understood the implications of what they were telling her because she kept repeating, 'Tell them to cut it out. I don't mind any pain. Tell them to cut it out.'

Eventually, the doctor left Henry and Penny alone. Henry sat in his chair, holding Penny's hand and struggling to stay calm. He had married Penny when she was barely 21 and he was in his late 30s. The end of his first marriage had left him bitter and exhausted. He had not meant to fall in love with Penny but her beauty and her gentleness had entranced him at a time when he was feeling vulnerable and unlovable. She restored his belief in himself and he had started to write again.

They had two girls – a third child was still-born. They named both girls after writers admired by Henry. Emily, the elder, and named after Emily Dickinson, had been born barely a year after they married but then there had been a gap before, first, Katherine (after Katherine Mansfield) and, then, the final, lost baby were born. It had been a conscious decision to wait until the household finances were healthier before expanding the family – Emily had arrived more by accident than design. Henry loved both his daughters, albeit in that rather distant way of fathers from his generation – but he worshipped Penny.

Henry never really got over his astonishment that someone as young and lovely as Penny loved him. He was a man who had been greatly disappointed by his experiences with women and, when war broke out in 1939, he had welcomed the chance to escape into the male, relatively uncomplicated world of the army. But, his military service was cut short by illness and, in the summer of 1944, he had met Penny, in the guise of nursing auxiliary, while he was convalescing in a military hospital.

To fall in love with your nurse is one of the oldest clichés in the book and the irony was not lost on Henry that he, a writer of fiction, should be caught in a plot development that he would have rejected out of hand for one of his own works. But, in spite of the banality of the situation, Penny and Henry did fall in love and were married two months after VE-Day on a warm July day at Kensington Registry Office. Penny's parents had not approved, partly because Henry was so much older than their young daughter but mainly because he was divorced.

Their early years together had been a struggle. After demobilisation, Henry found it difficult to find work. For several months, Penny was the only one who brought a regular income into the household as a secretary. Henry moonlighted for a while as a taxi-driver and tried, without success, to sell several short stories to magazines. The low household family income meant that the newly-weds could barely afford the tiny flat they rented at the top of a tall terraced house in West London. Penny had to haul coal up the four flights of stairs from the coal bunker because Henry was not strong enough, as a result of his wartime injuries, and the electricity and gas were supplied through ravenous coin meters.

Eventually, Henry had found a position with the Evening Mail as an assistant literary editor. Once he had managed to sell a few stories to a couple of national women's magazines, the commissions came in for more stories. The Stewarts moved slowly up the housing ladder until they were installed in a large rambling Victorian house in the outer suburbs.

As Henry held his wife's hand he reflected on the years they had spent together, the good times and the bad, and he feared the emptiness stretching out before him once she had gone.

Penny's decline was rapid. As there was nothing that could be done for her at the hospital, she came home. The local hospice, a pioneering institution, had an at-home nursing programme and relentlessly cheerful and patient nurses provided round-the-clock cover. The family took it in turns to sit with Penny, reading to her and playing music at first – but the drugs being given to Penny and the growing tumour combined very quickly to make it impossible for Penny to concentrate on anything for long. She moved fitfully between sleep and an uncomprehending consciousness. When someone tried to engage her in conversation, her eyes opened wide, staring into a distance far removed from the present. Occasionally she spoke but the words appeared to make little sense to the one or other of the Stewarts straining to catch them. Her beautiful face rapidly became swollen as a consequence of the drugs, her eyes grew dark and dull and her bodily functions all but collapsed.

It was a draining, harrowing time for everybody. Henry retreated to his study when he wasn't with Penny, cradling a drink, trying, and failing, to write. Emily busied herself, at first thinking up different kinds of food that might bring some temporary pleasure to Penny and cooking batches of grilled tomatoes or goujons of fish. But Penny could hardly eat anything and the fridge soon filled up with unwanted meals. Katherine spent many hours talking to Jane – or pretending to read about Delacroix.

The end came early one afternoon. The family had just finished lunch and Katherine was washing up, the radio playing in the background. Henry was still sitting at the table finishing his coffee. The nurses had left for an hour's break and Emily had taken up bedside duty. Suddenly, she rushed into the breakfast room.

'You'd better come. I think Mum's dead.'

Everyone stopped for a split second, frozen in fear. Then Henry moved rapidly towards the door and Katherine moved instinctively to turn off the radio. The Stewart family moved as one up the stairs and into the spare bedroom where Penny had spent the last 18 days of her life. She lay motionless, her eyes fixed open towards the ceiling. Henry collapsed onto the waiting bedside chair and held Penny's hand close to his face, tears sliding silently down his cheek, onto his hand and then hers. Emily turned and collapsed into Katherine's arms, choking on her sobs. Katherine did not cry. She gazed unblinking at the lifeless form on the bed and at her grieving father. Perhaps she was in shock, perhaps she was determined not to be weak, for the sake of everyone else. Whatever the reason, she stood there immobile, seemingly detached, holding her sister but not participating, holding herself in. The pain would have to wait.

A few days after the funeral, Katherine prepared for her return to Paris. Henry had insisted and, in truth, Katherine wanted to go back. She had no role to play in this suddenly motherless household. Emily would be able to keep Henry company when she wasn't at work. Paris, with all its drawbacks, would be a relief.

22

A new year

The staff and girls were very kind. Both Madame Grondin and Mademoiselle Mercier asked Katherine to their apartments for tea on consecutive Sundays and Josette and Anne-Marie clasped Katherine in their arms and hugged her close, saying that if there was anything they could do, she only had to ask. When she took her first classes after her return, the girls were subdued, uncertain how they should behave and not knowing what they should say. Katherine reassured each class that she was absolutely fine and hoped that they would all continue to work well at their English. Before too long, the usual pattern was re-established, including the meetings in the local café.

Not long after her return, Katherine called Patrick.

'Katherine, we've been worried about you. Why didn't you call sooner? How long have you been back in Paris?'

'A few days or so.'

'Look, come round this evening. We'll have a bite to eat and so on. Bring your bath things.'

Both Patrick and Terri hugged her hard and said how sorry they were about Penny.

'She was a remarkable person,' Patrick said. 'I have just written to Henry; he must be feeling quite desperate without her. She meant everything to him, you know. I think it will take him a long time to grieve.'

'Yes, I'm sure it will. But Emily's there. It could be worse.'

Katherine did not want to talk about Penny's death and didn't want to think about Henry. She felt some guilt at not being at home but also knew that she would be of little help if she were there.

Patrick and Terri told Katherine about Beirut, its elegant boulevards and pavement cafés, the hotel with its wonderful staff and heated swimming pool, the cocktails in the evening and the gourmet meals. They had had a good time. But now they were back in Paris, it was time for a clean-out of the system (Patrick's words.) They were going to embark on a five-day fast, starting Monday.

'It's something I've always done,' explained Patrick. 'Three or four times a year I just drink water, with maybe a little bilberry juice, for five days. It gives a complete shock to the system, cleans you out and leaves you feeling so alive. It's a wonderfully economical alternative to staying at a health farm. Why don't you do the same? I'm sure you'll find it an energising experience – and it's so good for you.'

Katherine was less than convinced that starving for five days could bring anything but hunger and discomfort. On the other hand, maybe this would be a way to lose weight (yet again) and if she did it with Terri and Patrick, she might just stick to it.

'Okay, what have I got to lose?' she answered eventually,

before realising the awfulness of the Freudian slip. They laughed before agreeing to meet up at the end of the week to find out how they were all doing.

As usual, Katherine returned home by metro. She enjoyed travelling on the Paris underground. It felt and smelt completely different from the London tube. At that time, the line that ran down to the 16th arrondissement still had carriages with wooden seats and floors – not a suspicion of plastic or leatherette to be seen. Katherine liked to travel in these throwbacks to a different age, when the signs asking that seats be given up for disabled war veterans, the '*mutilés de guerre*', had a real meaning. France still lived its history.

But the metro could be modern as well. Katherine loved the swooshing sound of the rubber wheels on the trains on line 1 when they pulled around the bend at Bastille station. These modern trains were elegant in their own way and remarkably quiet, a description that could scarcely be applied to the London Tube.

The underground stations too held much charm for Katherine. Each time she travelled on the metro she found something new to look at. Franklin Roosevelt was particularly bright and elegant, with glass display cases advertising the wares of the upmarket shops on the Champs Elysées, while Louvre reflected the riches of the museum above ground with examples of classical statues decorating its walls. Most of the stations were still dressed in their original clothes – thousands of white ceramic tiles lined the walls, wood-slatted escalators and ancient lifts connected the various levels and dusty advertisements for Dubonnet could still be glimpsed in the tunnels as the trains rushed past.

The difference between the advertising hoardings in the metro compared with those in London had struck Katherine the very first time she used the system. In London the Tube station walls were covered with a multiplicity of small adverts, each for something different. But in Paris the hoardings were huge and small in number – and worked on the principle of repetition. So, one station's walls might be covered with the same advertisement for a holiday company and the next might be showing endless images of a girl in DIM tights. Katherine became so used to this relentless parade of identical pictures that she came to view it as the norm and was temporarily shocked by the variety of advertising images that greeted her when she returned to London.

If the trains and the physical layout of the stations were distinctive, the smell was the essence of the metro. As people descended by stair or escalator below the ground, a hot, heady mix of dust, sweat, rubber, perfume, garlic and Gauloises hit their nostrils. It was a sweet, organic smell, quite unlike any other. A blind man would know immediately that he could only be in Paris.

So it was that Katherine returned to her room, surrounded by the images, smells and noises that had become so familiar and strangely comforting to her. Travelling on the metro was almost a badge of belonging, she knew the lines and where they led, which stations acted as interchanges and where she should ride on the train to be closest to the exit she needed. She was home.

23

Holding fast

When Katherine woke the next day, she had filled her little saucepan with water and turned on the electric ring before remembering that she had agreed to fast. She wondered whether an infusion would be acceptable and decided that it would, after all it was only water with a bit of extra colour. She put a bag into her mug and filled it almost to the brim. While the tilleul infused, she washed and put on her clothes. Then she sat on the edge of the bed and drank, very slowly. If she was not going to eat, she would make any liquid intake last as long as possible.

To avoid the temptation of the café on the Rue de Rivoli, she took the metro to school and, to avoid the temptation of school lunch, she went out of the lycée at lunchtime and took a walk along the river. By the time she had returned to her room in the late afternoon, she was very hungry. Several glasses of water, alternated with cigarettes, did not help. By early evening, she was feeling a bit dizzy. The only solution was to go to bed.

This set the pattern for the next four days. The hunger came and went and the number of daily infusions increased but Katherine stuck it out. She was able to report back to Patrick and Terri that she had indeed fasted for five days. The benefits were not obvious as she felt tired and lethargic – and empty. But both Patrick and Terri assured her that she looked much better for it and urged her to join them in the next fast later in the year. She agreed.

Perhaps five days' fast had been too brutal an introduction to the concept for Katherine's body. She could barely eat the food prepared by Terri to break their collective purge. She chewed a few mouthfuls of salad, nibbled on a couple of pieces of bread and played with her cheese. The wine went straight to her head. After drinking perhaps half a glass, she could feel the chemicals racing through her system. She was woozy and incoherent. Katherine made her excuses and left early.

Lying in her bed, Katherine found it impossible to get to sleep. In the darkness of her room, she listened to the water gurgling up through the pipes to the ancient radiator under her window. Occasional steps in the corridor outside heralded the return of other occupants of the chambres de bonne, which snaked in a long corridor around two sides of the attic floor. She was hot and sweaty and the sheets stuck to her body, making uncomfortable ridges under her back. Visions of Penny floated in and out of Katherine's consciousness as she turned restlessly this way and that, trying to blank out the dual images of her mother, the one alive and laughing, the other dead and pale as faded linen.

When she woke the next morning, Katherine was grateful to find that she no longer felt sick or headachy. Patrick had been careful to point out that lengthy fasts should be embarked upon only rarely but, as she sat on her bed drinking her morning infusion, Katherine rationalised that more frequent, shorter fasts would not harm someone such as herself, who had fat to spare. She decided that fasting every two weeks for a couple of days could be the answer to her hitherto hapless attempts at losing weight. She had done it once, so she could do it again.

24

Poor little rich girl

As she turned from locking her door, Katherine bumped into another young woman in the corridor just outside her chambre de bonne.

'I'm so sorry,' said the stranger. 'I couldn't see where I was going.'

This was because she was carrying a very large pile of bits of cloth – brightly coloured tweeds and satins, some pale calico and other materials Katherine couldn't immediately put a name to – and the odd ball of wool.

'It's for my collage,' she explained, seeing Katherine's questioning look. 'I'm studying at the Ecole des Beaux Arts.'

'I see,' said Katherine, though she didn't see at all.

'Oh, you must be Katherine. Maman's new English girl. I'm Beatrice Duval.'

Beatrice put down the pile and extended her hand; the young women shook.

'Come to my room – I'm just round the corner.'

Beatrice had inherited – or learnt – her mother's imperious manner such that this was less a suggestion than an order. Each took half of the pile and Beatrice led Katherine round the corner to the very last room on the floor.

'Come on in.'

This room was only a little wider than Katherine's but there the resemblance ended. Kilims covered the floor, the bed was dressed with velvet cushions and a contrasting bedspread, the walls could scarcely be seen for all the mirrors, paintings and photographs – and at the window end was an antique desk, covered in scraps of paper and cloth, lit by a tassel-shaded lamp.

'Have a seat.' Beatrice waved in the direction of the bed, after relieving Katherine of her half of the burden.

'I had to have a room of my own, to be independent from everybody else,' Beatrice explained. 'It's impossible to concentrate downstairs – the boys are such a nuisance and Maman just doesn't understand modern art. She's so bourgeoise – she thinks painting should have stopped with Renoir!'

Katherine was surprised to hear that Madame Duval took so narrow a view but then realised that almost all the paintings in the large salon were either portraits or still lifes. Neither an abstract nor anything remotely avant-garde in sight.

Beatrice carried on talking. 'How are you finding it, trying to teach the other two? They're so spoilt; I can't imagine it's any fun. The last English girl left after five weeks.'

So, that was why she had referred to her as the new English girl – though new, after several months, seemed to be stretching the point.

'Actually, I've not been able to give them much conversation at all – it seems they're never available when I am. But...' Katherine's voice trailed away; she had been on the verge of saying that that suited her just fine.

Beatrice jumped in. 'And I'll bet you're delighted. I shouldn't worry about it, if I were you. Maman is so busy, it'll be an age before she realises. And Yves will sweet-talk her out of insisting – he's good at that.'

'What about your father? Won't he mind?' asked Katherine, who had, in fact, neither seen nor heard anything about Mr Duval.

'Oh, he's hardly ever here. He's in the arms business, you know, so he's usually away during the week – busy selling to the highest bidder. And then, at the weekend, he and Maman go off to our place in the country, where he can shoot at birds or hunt some other poor defenceless creatures.'

Beatrice did not appear to have a very high opinion of her father.

'Of course, he makes a lot of money and that gives him the power. But as soon as I've finished my studies, I'm leaving here and going to set up in a studio somewhere and I won't take another cent from him.'

Katherine was shocked that Beatrice was talking about her father in this way – to a complete stranger. She got up to leave.

'You're not going yet are you? It's so good to have someone to talk to. You must stay a bit longer.'

Katherine sat down again, reluctantly.

'Where will you have your studio?' she asked.

'Oh, I don't know – it will have to be somewhere in the south. The light is so amazing on the Côte d'Azur. That's why Picasso lives there – and Léger had a studio in the same area. Oh and lots of other artists. Do you know Paloma Picasso? She's just wonderful – and designs the most incredible jewellery. There's someone who's been able to make her own way through her talent

– not because of who her father is.'

Katherine doubted whether this was completely accurate – she also wondered why Beatrice should imagine that she, Katherine, would know Paloma Picasso. This was no good – she could contribute nothing to this one-sided, name-dropping conversation.

'I really must go, Beatrice. It's been lovely to meet you.'

They shook hands and Katherine moved towards the door. Beatrice turned immediately to the pile of textiles sitting in the middle of the floor and didn't look up as Katherine left.

Outside, in the corridor, Katherine reflected on the fact that she had managed to live so long on the sixth floor and not realise that the daughter of the Duvals was camping out in a chambre de bonne. She hadn't even known that there was a daughter. Camping out was probably not quite the right expression – Katherine had no doubt that Beatrice didn't shower in the kitchen and suspected that she didn't indulge in too much bedsit cookery either. She was just a poor little rich girl, playing at being independent but all the while knowing that, if she needed to, she could always go downstairs where every civilised comfort was at hand.

25

Looking for inspiration

Max paced up and down in front of the canvas. He had been working on it for several weeks but the vision he had in his head was proving depressingly difficult to transfer into oils. The picture was intended as the centrepiece for an exhibition that Jocelyne had arranged for him. And the preview night, the vernissage, was only a few months away. If he could not complete the painting soon, the oil paints would have no time to dry out thoroughly – making transportation a problem.

Jocelyne had insisted on the exhibition, despite Max's best attempts to dissuade her. She had cajoled and charmed the gallery owner in equal measures to agree to it – and she was not going to take no for an answer, either from the gallery or, more importantly, from Max. He had tried every argument he could think of when Jocelyne first mentioned the possibility of a show – he wasn't ready for the critics; he didn't have enough paintings worthy of an exhibition; he was still developing his ideas. But Jocelyne in full flow was impossible to resist – and she did pay the bills.

Being a kept man increasingly bothered Max but, at the beginning of their affair, Jocelyne had made it so easy that he had willingly slipped into the role demanded of him – impoverished artistic genius saved by the love (and money) of a good woman. He had been in Paris for nearly 10 years when he first met Jocelyne – and, up to then, he had been forced to supplement the very meagre earnings from private sales of his paintings with taking what commercial work was available and giving art lessons to the untalented daughters of the Parisian bourgeoisie. Jocelyne's money made it possible for him to concentrate full-time on his own art.

Jocelyne had also acted as his muse and model for several paintings that had ultimately formed a series *Woman One* to *Woman Seven*. Jocelyne's friends had admired and bought these paintings, which now hung in various apartments both in Paris and the south of France. As Max's work moved further away from the figurative towards the abstract and surreal, the buyers had become thinner on the ground. Patrick's purchase of *The Night* had been one of few such sales in recent years – and even that had been at a reduced price 'for my dearest friend'. But Jocelyne remained convinced that Max simply needed to expose his work to a wider audience – and so the push towards a full exhibition was born.

As Max pondered his canvas and stared at his oil paints, Jocelyne swept in, depositing carrier bags of various shapes and sizes on the ground.

'I have been shopping,' she announced. 'And now I am quite exhausted,' she added, sinking into an armchair where she kicked off her shoes and stretched her feet in mid-air. 'Darling, you couldn't get me a glass of wine, could you?'

Max put down his brush and walked over to the small kitchen

and took a half-empty bottle of white wine from the fridge. There was just sufficient for two glasses, which he carried back towards Jocelyne, who had now draped herself across the chair, her legs dangling over the side.

'There, this should revive you.'

'Thank you, chéri.' Jocelyne sipped gratefully at the wine. 'Have you been making progress while I've been out?'

'No.' Max stood in front of her, staring down at the glass in his hand.

'Can you really not see where you are going with it? You seemed so sure when you started. Why is it so difficult to finish?'

Max's hesitation and lack of progress over the painting puzzled Jocelyne and also irritated her a little. She was the type of person who, having decided on a course of action, pursued it single-mindedly and with utter conviction. The idea that you could start something but not take it to completion was foreign to her. It felt to her almost as though Max were stalling deliberately – to prove that the exhibition had been a bad idea.

'I don't know. I really don't. There's too much black, not enough reds and oranges at the centre – but it just won't come together.'

'Well, why don't you start on something else and come back to this when you can look at it with a fresh eye.' Jocelyne was not sure she could take too many more days of Max staring at the canvas but doing nothing. Some activity, any activity, had to be better than his current state of nothingness.

'Yes, perhaps you are right. I'll start tomorrow.'

'Good. Oh, look at the time, I need to get ready. You haven't forgotten we're going to Patrick's this evening, have you?'

'What? Oh no, of course not.' Of course Max had forgotten but since he was not the one who needed an hour-and-a half to get changed, this did not seem particularly important.

The couple arrived at Patrick's flat on time, which is to say exactly 15 minutes late. The other invitees for the evening were already installed in the small sitting room with Patrick – Katherine, who had sat herself in one of the corners of the sofa, and Yvette, a photographer, who was curled up in the armchair and leafing through a book about Indian palaces. Terri fetched the latecomers some wine and handed them their glasses before settling on the arm of the chair where Patrick was sitting. Jocelyne sat in the free corner of the sofa close to Patrick, which meant Max had to squeeze between Jocelyne and Katherine.

'Good evening,' nodded Max politely at Katherine as he extended his hand in greeting. They shook hands and Katherine smiled and shifted slightly in her seat to give him more room.

'I hope you have enough room.'

'But, of course, how could I not, between two such beautiful ladies?' It was a careless compliment but, as he said it, Max looked at Katherine and, though they had met on several occasions at Patrick's, he felt as if he were really seeing her for the first time.

Katherine's regime of on-off fasting and regular, long walks meant that she had indeed lost weight and, with her hair pulled back, her eyes dominated a newly-revealed heart-shaped face. Max stared into the blue-green eyes opposite him, registering the length of her eyelashes, the darkness of her brows, the paleness of her skin. He felt a strange impulse to touch her cheek.

'Max, do you have my cigarettes?' Jocelyne's voice broke into the moment. He felt in his jacket and pulled out a pack of Camel. Jocelyne took one and held the cigarette to her mouth, waiting for Max to light it. He fumbled with the lighter, unable to get it to work.

'Oh, give it to me,' Jocelyne said in exasperation and she took the lighter from him. 'For an artist, you can be extraordinarily clumsy.'

Terri leapt from her perch and announced that supper must be ready. The group filed into the kitchen and settled around the table, where a first course of goat's cheese salad was already laid and the aromas of home-made vegetable moussaka were wafting from the oven. Patrick sat in his usual chair with his back to the door, Terri to his right and Jocelyne to his left. Katherine sat next to Jocelyne and opposite Yvette, with Max at the window end of the table.

More wine was poured, the salad eaten and then the vegetarian moussaka, which met with universal approval of its combination of aubergines, peppers and mushrooms. From his vantage point at one end of the table, Max could observe, without any apparent movement of his eyes, both Jocelyne and Katherine. Jocelyne gossiped gaily with Patrick and Terri, while Katherine volunteered little, replied when spoken to and spent most of the meal steadfastly concentrating on the food in front of her.

The contrast between the two women could not have been greater. Jocelyne's hair was cut in the latest style, her make-up perfectly applied, her clothes reassuringly expensive. Katherine's hair was held in a simple pony-tail, her make-up appeared to be no more than a dash of mascara and a dab of pink at the mouth (Katherine had learnt that less was more), and she was wearing a checked shirt and a pair of jeans. Max could feel himself admiring Jocelyne's style and elegance but all the while experiencing an almost overwhelming desire to reach out to the younger woman next to him.

A few stray hairs curled at the nape of her neck and Max wanted desperately to kiss the slender arc from Katherine's shoulder to her head.

Finally, Terri brought out a magnificent brie and a bowl of mixed black and green grapes, before moving to the cooker to put on the coffee. Patrick reached into a drawer and pulled out a couple of slabs of foil-wrapped bitter chocolate, which he broke into pieces and offered round.

Once they were all supplied with a small cup of dark coffee, chocolate and a glass of Armagnac, Patrick turned to Yvette.

'Now, my dear, you must tell us about this colour theory of yours.'

Yvette laughed and put down her cup. 'Well, it's nothing very spectacular. It's just that I see in colours. You know, it's a bit like Rimbaud – his giving colours to letters of the alphabet.'

Katherine thought back to her work on nineteenth century poets.

'Oh yes, I know – A noir, E blanc. That kind of thing.'

'Precisely. Except for me it is people who have colours. When I meet someone I see them as a colour – not necessarily the ones they dress themselves in or the colours they say they like the best. It's more a reflection of how I see their inner spirit, if that doesn't seem too precious.'

'I see, a bit like the auras that are supposed to surround us.'

'Yes, a bit like that.'

'So, what colour are you, Yvette?' asked Max.

'I? I am a burnt orange – lots of fire and earth mixed together.'

'And the rest of us?' asked Terri.

'Well, let me see,' Yvette looked around at the expectant faces.

Of course, everyone assembled around the table began to imagine what colours Yvette would ascribe to them and hoped that they would seem flattering or noble, at the very least not pink.

'OK, here goes.' Yvette turned towards Patrick. 'You, Patrick, are silver-grey – the colour of aeroplane bodies glinting in the sun, sophisticated, sharp, rather cool. And you, Terri, are a deep sea-green, almost turquoise – the sort of colour that shifts as it moves, changes colour depending on the light. Jocelyne is scarlet, a strong, you might almost say angry, red - and Max, dear Max, you are blue, a very dark blue – like the night – almost purple.'

All eyes then turned to Katherine.

'And me? Do I have a colour?' she asked.

'Ah, but of course, and, yet, you are not a single colour,' replied Yvette. 'You are a bright, sunshine yellow – but with black spots.'

26

Female intuition

Jocelyne was not happy when she and Max returned to their apartment after Patrick's dinner party.

'You couldn't take your eyes off her,' she exclaimed as they came through the door, speaking for the first time since they had said their goodbyes to Patrick and Terri.

'Who?'

'Katherine, the little mouse.'

'Oh, don't be absurd. I wasn't looking at her any more than anybody else. You're imagining things.' Max wondered to himself how it was that women always knew these things, no matter how carefully a man might try to conceal his thoughts or actions.

'I am not – I saw you when we were eating. Just because she's young and has big eyes. I don't suppose she's as innocent as she looks – after all, she introduced Patrick to Terri.'

There was no answering the distorted logic. Jocelyne had been convinced from when Terri first moved in with Patrick that she was up to no good, and had said as much to Patrick, who had in turn made it very clear that he would not countenance any criticism of his new companion. Jocelyne valued her friendship with Patrick and, so, had said nothing further to him – but Max was only too aware of her views.

'Look, this is all nonsense. I am not interested in Katherine – but neither do I believe that she can be held responsible for her friend. Come on, I'm tired - let's go to bed.'

'No, that's your answer to everything. You are not going to dismiss this just like that. I know what I saw. You have to promise me that you won't try to see that girl.'

Max stared at Jocelyne, trying to think of something useful he could say. It had not occurred to him to do anything so active as try and see Katherine. She had disturbed him that evening but he hadn't thought further than that their paths might cross again at another of Patrick's evenings. But even that thought was, if he was honest, disloyal to Jocelyne. He owed her too much.

27

Chance encounter

Katherine was late for her first class at school and, head down, was walking very fast and determinedly towards the Metro. She did not notice the man coming towards her, equally distracted as he pondered how to tell Jocelyne that the final piece would definitely not be ready in time. Naturally, they collided.

'Oh, excuse me,' stammered Katherine. 'I'm so sorry. I wasn't looking where I was going.'

'Neither was I,' replied Max, smiling happily at the flustered girl. 'How are you, Katherine?'

Katherine, who had been struggling to keep hold of her book and papers looked up to see Max looking down at her. She flushed involuntarily.

'You seem to be in a hurry,' continued the painter amiably. 'Where are you off to?'

'School, I'm going to be late for my first class.'

'Where is that?'

'St Paul.'

'Really? What a coincidence, I've an appointment near there later this morning. When do your classes finish? We could meet for a coffee – there's a cafe just next to the metro station. It would make a nice change to have a chat other than at Patrick's. You know, get to know each other better.'

'I'm not sure,' began Katherine, trying to find a reason to say no, without really knowing why she wanted to refuse. But then she thought better of it. 'No, that would be lovely. I finish at 11.40, so we could meet at about 10 to 12, if that fits in with your plans.'

'Perfect. I'll see you at the café – you know which one? The little one immediately opposite the metro steps? Good, till then.'

Katherine hurried down into the Metro, leaving Max to reflect on his foolishness. He had no appointment near St Paul – and he was doing precisely what Jocelyne had asked him not to do. *Tant pis*, fate had decided otherwise.

The café was busy but Max had secured a table near the window and watched as Katherine approached. His artist's eye appraised her from head to foot. She walked well, head up, back straight. The wind was tugging at her shirt, outlining her curves. Her hair, gathered into a high ponytail, was swinging in time with her walk. She seemed to embody youth and confidence.

Max was unaware that Katherine had caught sight of him in the window as she walked towards the café, and consequently had pulled herself up and breathed in, trying to reassure herself that her inner anxieties were not showing.

'Hello again,' Max extended his hand in greeting. They shook and Katherine sat down. After the coffees had arrived – black for Max, a *petit crème* for Katherine – Max asked her about the school, how many classes she had, whether she enjoyed the teaching. Katherine in turn asked about his painting and whether the exhibition works were ready (Jocelyne had spoken at Patrick's at some length about the trials of putting on the show). Neither mentioned Jocelyne by name.

Katherine was enjoying the conversation. Max, with his heavily-accented French and ready smile, was far more charming than she had realised. He for his part was struck by his companion's engaging personality, which she seemed to hide when at Patrick's. More to the point, he found himself gazing at her neck, the whisps of hair curling around her forehead, her penetrating eyes.

'You know, Katherine, you are a very lovely girl,' Max could not help saying. 'Why are you so unsure of yourself?'

Katherine was taken aback. The conversation had veered abruptly from a neutral social exchange to something altogether different.

'Am I? I don't think so – it's just that. No, wait, why are we talking about this?', she floundered.

'Because, as I said, you are very lovely and you should have the confidence to show the world what you are – not hide yourself away as though you were a little mouse.'

Une petite souris: it sounded almost romantic.

'I think I should paint you – show you what you really are.'

Max had spoken without thinking. How could he paint this girl? Jocelyne would be more than furious. But, somehow, he did not care.

'Paint me? You want me to be your model?' Katherine was genuinely shocked, if flattered, at the suggestion.

'Yes, yes. I see it now. This could be the answer – you are my final piece.' Max leant back in his chair, feeling as though a great weight had been lifted from his shoulders. The answer had been there all the time – this strangely uncertain young woman would provide the inspiration he needed. The show could go ahead;

Jocelyne would be happy; he would be happy. Whether the girl would be happy did not cross his mind.

'Your final piece?'

'Not final as in for ever. The final piece for the show. My problem has been that I just could not see how to create my last, central piece – how to bring everything else together. And, to put it simply, you are the answer. It won't be a portrait in the conventional sense but rather an impression of you, your essence – the black and the yellow that Yvette so rightly talked about.'

'I see. Will Jocelyne know it's me?' Katherine's female intuition told her that Jocelyne was unlikely to be ecstatic at the thought of her posing for Max.

'Perhaps – but she doesn't have to – I can borrow a friend's studio for our sittings. All Jocelyne need know is that I have at last found the key.' Once again, Max found himself wondering yet again how it was that women so unerringly tapped into the unspoken thoughts of men.

'Well, I'm very flattered, of course. I'll think about it – but you should know now I'm not prepared to sit without any clothes on; that would just be too embarrassing.'

'No, no, of course not. It never entered my mind, I assure you,' replied Max, apparently without hesitation, internally with more than a little regret.

'Alright, I'll do it – if you're really sure.'

The deal had been struck; Katherine would become the artist's muse.

28

Holding back

Easter was fast approaching and Katherine knew she must go home for at least some of the holiday. The few times she had phoned from the local café, her father had steadfastly talked about nothing in particular, other than to say how pleased he was she had phoned and how busy he was with his work.

Katherine's letters home were self-consciously cheerful, full of amusing anecdotes about school, the latest visit to Patrick's and the art exhibitions she had been to. She did not write about Terri and Patrick nor about her modelling for Max. She certainly did not write about any of the men who had drifted in and out of her Parisian life.

Her father, meanwhile, sent short and witty letters, punctuated by doodles of him seeking inspiration for his latest short story, and progress reports on Emily's quest to get him to eat properly. Very occasionally he might mention Penny, as in, 'Your mother would have loved the garden just now,' but that was as far as he would go in acknowledging the aching void left by her death.

Katherine knew that her father must be terribly lonely and wished he could find it in himself to open up more about how he felt. On the other hand, she was not at all sure that she could cope with such emotion from a parent who up till then had always been slightly remote and with whom conversations had tended to revolve around the theoretical or academic rather than the realities of day-to-day life. If she was honest with herself, she was not looking forward to the trip.

The day before she was due to leave, Madame Duval sent word that she'd like to see her. Katherine hoped she didn't want to talk about the increasingly infrequent English lessons.

'You are going to London tomorrow, is that right?' asked Madame Duval.

'Yes, I'm on the 11.15 from Beauvais.'

'Good, good. I wonder if you could do me a favour while you are in England?'

'What would you like me to do?'

'Well, could you buy me a copy of *The Vivisector* by Patrick White? Have you heard of it? He's Australian, I believe, but apparently the story is about art and the struggle to be an artist. I can't get hold of it here – and I'd like to read it. Maybe I'll be able to understand what drives Beatrice a little better.'

'Oh, of course, no problem.' Katherine was agreeably surprised that Madame Duval was being so open; hitherto any remarks addressed to her by Madame Duval during their infrequent conversations had been business-like and impersonal, verging on glacial.

'Now, let me see,' Madame Duval opened her handbag and took out a slim, snakeskin wallet. 'I don't have much English currency. Do you mind if I give you a 50 pound note? I don't suppose you've seen one before.'

Katherine flushed at the unthinking rudeness of the woman. The hint of warmth in their conversation disappeared.

'That would be quite alright,' Katherine replied coolly, taking the proffered note. 'I'll make sure to bring you the correct change when I return.'

29

Changes

'You're looking great,' were Emily's first words. 'Have you been dieting?'

'Maybe, a bit,' Katherine mumbled back; she hadn't told any of her family about the fasting, and she did not want to get into the discussion with Emily.

'Well, whatever you've been doing, it's working.'

'How's Dad?'

'Bearing up. You know what he's like – it's impossible to tell what's really going on in his head but I think he's coping OK.'

Emily turned to the kitchen to put the kettle on while Katherine made her way up the stairs to her father's study and knocked on the door before going in.

'Katie, how wonderful to see you. Come in and give your father a hug.'

Katherine crossed over the floor and greeted her father with the requested hug and a kiss on the cheek.

'Have you seen Emily? She's probably making tea – it's her answer to most things.' Henry sat back in his chair and smiled at his younger daughter. 'I expect wine is more the order of the day in Paris.' He paused for a second or two, as though searching for his words. 'Penny enjoyed her glass of wine.'

'Are you alright, Dad?' asked Katherine, already disconcerted by how much he seemed to have aged in just a few months.

'I'm fine, just fine. Oh lord, is that the time? I must finish this story today – so, off you go, and we'll chat later. So lovely that you're home.' And with that, Henry waved Katherine away and looked back at his typewriter with its half-completed page.

Emily was waiting downstairs in the kitchen with two mugs of tea and an open packet of digestive biscuits.

'So, how do you find him?'

'Older, almost smaller. Has he talked to anybody? You know, a counsellor or someone?'

'Don't be daft. Do you honestly think Dad would open up to anyone like that? He just works all the time. I come round as often as I can but he hardly ever mentions Mum even though I'm sure he's thinking about her nearly all the time. He can be so damned British, stiff upper lip, sometimes. But what about you? How are you coping?'

'OK, I think. It's easier for me as I'm not here all the time, with so many things or places to remind me of Mum all the time. But every now and then I feel very sad, knowing I'll never be able to speak to her again. At least I'm not dreaming about her any more.'

'You've dreamt about her too? It's awful isn't it? You dream about her and everything's great – and then you wake up and she's gone. I had that a lot for the first few weeks.'

Katherine nodded in agreement; it wasn't worth trying to

explain that her mother had tended to be the lead role in nightmares rather than Utopian visions of how it used to be.

Easter came and went. After Emily returned to her own flat, the days passed uneventfully. Henry worked in his study most of the time; Katherine made tea and coffee or prepared meals from her limited repertoire – spaghetti, salad, roast chicken. Henry made polite noises but Katherine knew it compared unfavourably with the marvels that Penny used to whip up seemingly out of nothing.

Jane invited Katherine over to spend the day with her family. Mr and Mrs Pendleton kissed Katherine warmly and said how sorry they had been to hear of her mother's death; Jane's sister Louise (14 going on 25) asked her about Paris fashions.

Katherine and Jane spent a happy day catching up (unlike with her sister, Katherine told Jane everything) and then Jane's boyfriend Harry dropped by and the three of them went off to the local pub.

The Dragon Arms had been a coaching inn in an earlier existence. Sandwiched incongruously between a dry cleaners, *We put the Art into smArt*, and an estate agents, *The rental's* [sic] *experts*, the pub could, in a different context, have doubled as a Dickensian inn, with its huge wooden doors leading to a cobbled alleyway that broadened out into one of the largest pub gardens in north London and its warren of wood-panelled rooms inside. The massive fireplace at the front, which crackled enthusiastically in the winter months, was empty but the pub managed to retain an air of old-world charm.

Harry elbowed his way through the crowd with gin and tonic for the girls and a pint of John Smith's for himself. He paused for a moment before reaching the table: the girls were deep in conversation and were taking no notice of their waiter so he was able to observe them both.

Jane was her usual, familiar self with her bleached-blonde hair (she hadn't been her natural mid-brown since her mid-teens) framing a striking if not conventionally pretty face, which remained largely impassive regardless of the topic under discussion. Jane's fierce intellect and straightforward pragmatism were what had attracted Harry to Jane, even at school. And here she was, doubtless dispensing sound advice to their companion, judging by the keen attention Katherine was paying to Jane's every word.

Katherine, on the other hand, had changed. If he was honest, Harry had always felt a certain attraction for Katherine – but now he sensed a certain danger in the easy companionship between the three of them. Her long, brown hair fell down over her shoulders and masked the side of her face but he could still make out the curl of her lashes (he hadn't noticed before just how long they were) and her hands kept straying from her sides as she emphasised a particular point in a noticeably continental way. She seemed suddenly exotic and desirable and he was not sure that this was simply because they hadn't seen each other for a while, nor even because she was a fair bit slimmer than she had been. He wasn't as shallow as that, was he?

'So, where does all this modelling take place, then?' Jane was asking as Harry put the drinks down on the table.

'At a friend's studio. A friend of Max's, that is. It's not far from school, so we can fit in sessions quite easily,' replied Katherine, reaching for her drink and accidentally brushing against Harry's hand.

'Mm,' was the response from Jane, who was surprised to see that Harry appeared to be blushing. 'And you say that what's her name, Jocelyne, knows nothing about all this?'

'Well, I'm pretty certain she doesn't know anything. She's incredibly possessive of Max and I don't think she likes me very much at all. So, it's better this way.'

'Mm, and what do you think is going to happen when he unveils this picture? Do you think she's really not going to know that it's you?'

'I'm just hoping that Max keeps to his end of the bargain and she won't be able to tell. But, if she does, it'll be too late by then and I'll just have to deal with it.'

This last surprised but pleased Jane – Katherine, the least confrontational being she had ever known, appeared to be learning that sometimes you can't run away, you have to stand your ground.

'Well, good for you. So, presumably, there's nothing between you and Max, nothing that could compromise your position, if Jocelyne does go off at the deep end?'

'No, of course not,' replied Katherine, perhaps a shade quickly. 'I'm simply the channel enabling him to complete his show. That's all.'

'Mm.'

'So, who's this Max person, then?' asked Harry, who had, of course, missed the beginning of this particular part of the conversation.

'Oh, he's just an artist, a friend of Patrick's. He asked me to model for him.'

'I gathered that much. But why did he ask you? Surely Paris is crawling with artists' models?'

'It's not that simple. You see, he'd got stuck and couldn't finish his final piece for a show he's having and then a friend at Patrick's gave us all colours – and mine were yellow and black. And Max suddenly realised that that was what he needed and, so, he needed me.' Katherine could sense that this was not a particularly coherent explanation – but it would have to do.

'Well, I don't see but then I'm not an artist, just a plain old physicist. Speaking of which, I trust you realise what a sacrifice Jane and I are making by going out with you – instead of revising? It's alright for you but we've got Finals next term!'

They all laughed and the conversation moved on. Last orders came and went and the three of them tumbled out of the pub with the rest of the stragglers into the chill night air.

'Jane, I'll drop you off first and then take Katherine home, if that's OK.'

'Makes sense to me. I'm tired anyway so it'll be good to get home now.'

Harry dropped off Jane with a kiss and a promise to phone the next day and then he drove Katherine home.

'Is there really nothing going on with you and this Max person?' asked Harry as he drew the car up to the kerb.

'No, of course there isn't, he's old enough to be my father. Well, he would be if my father were more typical. Anyway, what would it matter if there was anything going on?'

'It's just I wouldn't want you to get hurt. I don't like the idea,' Harry hesitated. 'I don't like the idea of you getting mixed up with someone who's clearly just using you for his own ends. You're not like Terri; she'll walk away from Patrick when the time comes and not look back. It'll just be one more experience to cross off her list – but you're different. If you let yourself become involved, it'll be you that suffers in the end.'

This was probably the most personal that Harry had ever been with Katherine and she was disconcerted by his concern. She looked at him carefully, trying to understand why he was being so protective.

'I'll be fine, Harry. Don't worry,' was all she found to say. She leant across to kiss Harry goodnight on the cheek but he turned his head at just the wrong moment and their lips met. Both pulled away, embarrassed.

'Goodnight, Harry,' Katherine said firmly as she opened the car door and shut it quickly after her. He watched her go into her house and then drove away.

30

Light and dark

Back in Paris, the sittings for Max were at his friend Henri's studio, tucked away in the rue des Templiers. The few sessions they had managed before Easter had left Max with some charcoal and pen-and-ink sketches of Katherine. These were mainly of her head and shoulders though some simply captured the line of her profile or the arc of her neck, drawn in isolation without the distraction of a face attached to it. All the sittings had been, as Katherine had insisted, fully-clothed.

This did not prevent, possibly encouraged, Max to imagine Katherine without her clothes. It was too frustrating only to be able to capture part of her essence. At least that's how he rationalised his feelings to himself. He decided that after she returned from London he would suggest she should reveal more of herself, in the interests of art.

'Have you seen any of Ingres' paintings at the Louvre?' Max asked as he busied himself sorting out brushes and inks.

'I've certainly seen some of them. His women seem to be incredibly soft, as though they had been poured into place.'

As usual, and by now he should have known better, Max was slightly taken aback by Katherine's knack of getting to the heart of things.

'Indeed. That is exactly so – poured into place, like creamy milk. You know, when he first exhibited his Grande Odalisque he came in for much criticism because of the lack of true proportion – they said he had distorted her body so much that it was not a true representation and therefore bad art.'

'But I think his paintings are beautiful.'

'So, do I – but critics are always way behind the artists in understanding new ways of looking.'

'Like they were with the impressionists.'

'Absolutely.'

Max continued to rearrange his tools.

'Anyway, I have been thinking about how Ingres captures his subjects, how he so often has the head turned and the neck exposed and leading so effortlessly to the shoulders and back. I think I should paint you like that – or at least the idea of you. What do you think?'

Katherine replied cautiously, 'How do you mean?'

'Well, first, I'd like you to take your hair away from your neck with a turban or a scarf – and then perhaps you could sit with your back to me and look over your shoulders, which should be bare. In fact, and obviously, only if you agree, perhaps you could sit with a gown falling away from your shoulders. So, we get the contrast between the colour of the scarf, the direct look of your eyes and the unbroken line of your shoulders and back. I need to start with that vision in front of me – but the end result will be very different. A line here, a block of colour there – the idea of light and dark,' Max's voice trailed away. It didn't sound very convincing even to him.

'OK.'

Max was momentarily nonplussed.

'Are you sure?'

'Not really but I think we know each other well enough by now, don't we? If you say it's what you need, then let's do it.'

'Good, good,' Max tried not to sound too eager. 'Let me fetch you something from Henri's props box and we'll get going.'

Some minutes later, Katherine was sitting on a box, her hair hidden under a yellow silk scarf tied up like a turban. She had changed behind a screen, taking off her top and bra and wrapping a length of sheeting around her. Once seated, she had eased the sheeting off her shoulders, holding it tightly in front of her. Max moved to pull the sheeting further down, so that it fell into an oval drop halfway down her back, exposing her shoulder blades. He could sense the tension in Katherine as she held on to the cloth – and he could sense the clamminess in his hands as he rearranged the sheet.

Max moved away and stood behind his easel to take a better look. He was shocked to realise how beautiful her back was – smooth and pale, blemish-free, soft and sensual. All the more exciting because it was evident that Katherine herself had no awareness of its impact.

'Turn your head over your left shoulder and look at the easel,' he directed.

Katherine's almond-shaped eyes immediately opened wide as she focused on the easel. Their direct, almost challenging look reminded Max of Vermeer more than Ingres. He paused briefly and then began to sketch in charcoal – hesitantly at first but as the minutes passed his strokes became more positive and he threw off sketch after sketch. A long line here, a curve there, a detailed study of the neck and shoulder blades, multiple renditions of the eyes, a heavily shaded sketch of everything – head, neck, back. Max worked almost feverishly, as though if he stopped he would lose for ever the inspiration in front of him.

After an hour, Katherine asked if she could move her head – her neck was beginning to stiffen up. Max put down his charcoal.

'Oh yes, of course. I am so sorry – you should have said something sooner. We can stop for a bit – you must be tired.'

'I am rather. Can we call it quits for today? I have to go soon anyway. Mademoiselle Mercier has called a pre-term planning meeting for the English department – and I really should go.'

This was not entirely true – Madame Grondin had sent Katherine a note about the meeting but had also said that it was optional for her to attend.

The moment of magic – at least that was how Max would think of it - was over. Katherine put her clothes back on behind the screen, handed Max the scarf and sheet and picked her jacket up from a chair.

'Will you come again – next week?' asked Max as he saw her to the door.

'Perhaps. I'll let you know.'

Katherine turned her head to kiss Max goodbye on the cheek. He took hold of her by the shoulders and pulled her closer, his dark eyes desperately searching hers for some sign that she too had felt that something had changed that afternoon. Katherine returned his gaze for a split second before wriggling out of his hold.

'I must go, Max.' She laughed nervously, quickly pecked at his cheek and left. He could hear her almost running down the stairs as he stood rooted to the spot. His heart was pounding and he could feel beads of sweat trickling down from his forehead. He turned to look back at the easel. The lines on the last sheet were very black, urgent, chaotic. He realised that it was actually true - he had found what he was looking for. The maddening, unobtainable English girl had given him the key.

31

Pierre

Although Katherine had become reasonably skilful at deflecting unwanted attention in the street, she never really got to grips with how to say no. The best way to deal with it would have been to let off a torrent of abuse in English and to refuse to engage in any French dialogue. But that would mark her out as a foreigner – and Katherine took great pride in her French. She wanted to be thought a native, not a visitor.

One Saturday afternoon, Katherine decided to walk to the Boul' Mich. There were some good student bookshops there and she hoped to find some cheap editions of books she needed for the next year's work back at college. It was a grey, miserable day with a fierce wind but she opted to walk the whole way, rather than take the metro, and battled, head down, against the elements along the Rue de Rivoli as far as Châtelet where she turned right to cross the river. As she made her way across, she could sense someone drawing level with her, and she steeled herself to repel all advances.

'Cheer up,' said a male voice. 'Where are you going with such a long face?'

Katherine turned involuntarily towards the speaker. He was short, dressed completely in black, had long dark hair and large spectacles and reminded her of Woody Allen. She smiled in spite of herself.

'Oh, just to the Boul' Mich,' she replied, breaking the first rule – don't get drawn into conversation.

'So am I. Are you a student?'

'I'm an assistante d'anglais.'

'Really? Well you speak very good French, just like a Parisian.'

'Oh, thank you. It's kind of you to say so,' Katherine said, breaking the second rule – never accept a compliment.

Before too long, the conversation had opened out and Katherine and Pierre were busy asking each other questions. Pierre was working on a thesis about the downfall of Trotsky. He came from Toulouse, where he had studied for his first degree and he lived in the north of Paris. Katherine had to speed up her typically slow walking speed to keep up with Pierre who walked very fast indeed for someone so small.

The two of them went, inevitably, into a café and had a drink. Equally inevitably, he invited her back to his place. She said yes.

They took the metro to Simplon. It was dark by the time they reached street level again. The area was poorly lit and the road steep. They walked up the hill for some ten minutes before turning into a modern block of flats. Pierre opened the main door and called the lift. They travelled up to the fourth floor and he opened the door to the flat. As Katherine stepped in behind him she caught sight of a young woman bending over a record player and dressed only in her bra and knickers.

'That's Corinne,' explained Pierre. 'We share the flat.'

Corinne had short, bobbed brown hair and was very slim – underwear suited her. She offered Katherine a cigarette.

'If you ever come here alone,' she said as she settled back on a cushion, 'do as I do. This is not a good area and you need to be careful. So, as soon as you come out of the metro, light a cigarette. That way you can defend yourself. A cigarette in the eye is a pretty good answer to most things.'

Katherine had not thought of cigarettes as an offensive weapon before. The day was turning out to be unusual in more ways than one.

'Do you like Brassens or Brel?'

'Well, I've heard them on the radio but I don't know their work that well.'

'OK, crash course coming up.'

Pierre sifted through the albums on the floor and first selected an early Brassens disc.

'This one is just sublime. He is a poet, you know, rather than a singer.'

They sat on the cushions listening to Brassens, and then Brel, and then more Brassens. They drank black coffee, as the milk in the fridge had gone off, and some wine. Corinne disappeared and got dressed to go out. Katherine and Pierre were left alone and Pierre led her into his room.

Like the rest of the flat, Pierre's room was a jumble, with cushions, clothes and books tossed in random piles on any available space. He undressed himself quickly and indicated she should do the same. As she took off her clothes, Katherine couldn't help thinking about Corinne in her tiny underwear and her sylph-like body. How could Pierre find her attractive when he lived with someone so sexy? She felt inadequate and dull and wished that she had not put on such sensible knickers and such an ancient bra that morning. Pierre, however, didn't seem to notice anything amiss but beckoned her on to the bed.

He took off his glasses and the two of them stared into each other's eyes for a brief moment.

'What do you like?' he asked.

She panicked slightly. You didn't ask what people liked; you just did it and hoped it was OK.

'I don't know. Anything,' she murmured.

He took her hands and kissed them and then proceeded to explore her with his hands and his tongue. He turned her over and stroked her back and then turned her forward again and traced a line from her neck, over her breasts and stomach down to her fur. She was excited and wet. He entered her and she squealed involuntarily. He came too quickly and she was disappointed but then he massaged her expertly and patiently until she too came and they both collapsed into the bed.

She had been dozing in the warmth for perhaps two minutes when he turned to her and said, 'You are on the Pill, aren't you?'

'Well, actually, I was but not any more.'

'Dear God, well have you got a douche?'

For a split-second, she wondered why she should have a shower with her and looked at him uncomprehendingly.

'There's one in the bathroom. You do know how to use it, don't you?'

'Oh, yes. Of course.'

She moved out of the bed, through the corridor to the tiny bathroom. There, on top of a basket, was what looked like a strange if rather small hot water bottle. Katherine took it between her hands and concluded that the only way to use it must be to fill it with water and somehow flush out her system. She filled it with some tepid water and squeezed the contents awkwardly into her opening, letting everything then drain away into the loo. She repeated the exercise a couple more times and dried herself off.

'Alright?' called out Pierre. 'Come back to bed now.'

Obediently, Katherine returned and the two of them fell asleep.

The following morning, Corinne was already up when Katherine emerged from the bedroom. She waved her towards the coffee pot in the kitchen and Katherine poured herself a cup – it was very bitter and barely warm. Corinne had on a wrap that skimmed her thighs and was more open than closed, revealing her breasts underneath. She appeared to have no self-consciousness whatsoever. Katherine envied her that and thought to herself what a joy it must be to be so secure in your own body.

Katherine contemplated taking a shower but felt that all she really wanted to do was leave as quickly as was decent. So, she agreed to meet Pierre at a café in the Latin Quarter the following evening and let herself out.

She kept the appointment and enjoyed the conversation. Pierre had lots of stimulating ideas about politics, literature and the tradition of the French chanson. He could be amusing and intense by turn. He was interesting. But, and it was a big but, she had felt uncomfortable at the apartment. She was uncertain about the relationship between Pierre and Corinne – and uncertain how she felt about him. Was it worth the unease, the douching, the feelings of inadequacy, of being out of her depth? Better to finish now, when she hardly knew him.

After the third glass of wine, she explained that she felt it would be better if they didn't see each other again. Pierre looked slightly surprised.

'Wasn't it good yesterday? I thought we were good together.'

'Yes, no, it isn't that. It's just... I don't think it's going to work out. I'm sorry.'

'My dear Katherine, when you get over your bourgeois inhibitions, you will have a wonderful life.'

Pierre tossed down a few francs to pay for the drinks, left quickly and disappeared from view among the crowds. Katherine walked towards the river and decided to cross by the Pont Neuf. Stopping halfway across she leaned against the wall and looked towards Notre Dame. The cathedral's huge flying buttresses were silhouetted against an indigo sky. The beauty of the view, as always, did not fail to impress her but she caught herself thinking how little the perfection of the buildings was matched by the lives of the people.

32

Un homme et une femme

'Mademoiselle,' the concierge called after Katherine. 'Someone came to see you this morning. I told her you were out and she should try later.'

'Did she give her name?'

'No. I don't know anything more,' the concierge replied in a tone of voice that clearly implied she had no interest in Mademoiselle's visitors.

Katherine had no idea who the caller might be. Terri never came round; the teachers at school didn't know where she lived. It was a small but intriguing mystery. But not for long – later that afternoon there was a quiet knock on her door and the open door revealed Janice, a fellow linguist who had landed a posting as assistante d'anglais in Compiègne.

Janice's visit was surprising on two counts – they were not close friends and, the last time they had been together at college, they had had what can only be described as an animated conversation about God. Janice was a true believer and paid-up Evangelical Protestant member of the God Squad. Katherine, who had toyed with religion in her teens, was, at best, agnostic and, when it came to debating the point with the likes of Janice, a confirmed atheist. Janice, astounded that someone could have read the bible and still not believe, had eventually left Katherine's room – frustrated, red-faced and muttering under her breath, 'If you hear the word of God and reject it, you must know you are condemned.'

'Janice, so it was you! Come in. How are things?'

Janice perched gingerly on the bed, putting her over-large bag down on the floor.

'Oh, great. I just thought I should visit Paris as it's so close by and, then, I thought I'd pop in and see how you were doing. This is a fantastic location. You must be so pleased to be right in the centre though this room is really quite small.......,' Janice tailed off as she took in the sparse surroundings.

'Small and not perfectly formed,' replied Katherine cheerily. 'How long have you been in town?'

'Oh, I came up yesterday – I'm staying in a hostel run by the Evangelical Church of Paris. Which is great as it's very cheap. I went to the Louvre this morning after trying to find you and then came along here to see if you were back.'

'Well, here I am. What would you like to do?'

After some discussion and perusal of the invaluable *Pariscope*, they decided to eat out on the Left Bank and then go to Le Champo cinema for a screening of *Un homme et une femme*, which was doing the rounds on re-release but which neither had seen.

Despite their differences, the two had an enjoyable meal in a small and unpretentious bistro popular with students and young office workers alike. While Janice tucked in to her steak and chips and Katherine her magret de canard, the two of them gossiped about friends in Oxford – though the ones that Janice knew most about held, it must be admitted, little interest for Katherine – and exchanged experiences of teaching in the French school system. Janice was working in a college rather than a lycée so her pupils were younger – between the ages of 11 and 15 – and their level of English accordingly lower.

'But most of them are very sweet and really try hard,' said Janice. 'At first, I was disappointed to be going to a small town rather than Paris or Toulouse but now I'm glad because I've really got to know the place and the people are usually much friendlier. And at weekends I go cycling in a club and, of course, on Sundays there's church. The minister's really dynamic and there are loads of events all year round. You should come and visit.'

Cycling and God were probably not the attractions most likely to lure Katherine from the capital but she nodded in a vaguely positive fashion.

Le Champo turned out to be a classic cinema from the golden age with an Art Deco façade and comfortable velvet seats. The film weaved its magic on the audience, including Janice, who, as far as Katherine knew, had never had a romantic liaison of any kind, and Katherine herself, who was entranced by it all – plot, photography, music – everything seemed ultra-sophisticated, ultra-cool. If only men like Jean-Louis Trintignant – or at least the role he played - existed in real life. But then, you probably had to look like Anouk Aimée to attract them. She pondered fleetingly over why he would say to her on the phone 'Je vous aime' rather than the more intimate 'Je t'aime' – yet another example of the subtle nuances of the language.

The young women parted with an embrace and a promise to keep in touch while they were both still in France.

As Katherine climbed the stairs to her chambre de bonne,

the music from the film still resonating in her mind, she reflected that it had been a good evening and that Janice had been good company, even though they would clearly never be friends in the way that she and Jane were friends. But next year, there would be few people left in college that Katherine knew well – so, staying in touch with Janice could ensure at least one friendly face the following autumn.

33

Losing it

Look at the diary of almost any young (and not so young) woman, and you will often find a recurring mark on a particular day of each month. This mark may be an asterisk, a discreet P or C (for curse) or even a name, such as Fred or Bert. Tracking her established monthly cycle, each woman knows when her next period should fall.

Katherine used the asterisk approach. It was easy for her to keep track because her body followed an exceptionally regular cycle – without fail, every four weeks, minor cramps would be followed by that unmistakeable warm but irksome flow. But, some time after she had finished with Pierre, she realised that she was late.

She went to school in the morning, hoping that her system would right itself by evening. But nothing happened. By the third late day, Katherine had to recognise the awful possibility that she was pregnant.

There was no way she could have a baby. It would ruin her university career, dismay her father. And there was no way she could tell anyone. She thought back to the girl at school who had fallen pregnant when just about to take her O levels. One day, she was at school; the next day, she had gone – never to be mentioned again by any member of staff nor, even, by any of the girls. She simply became a non-person.

Katherine realised she had only herself to blame – whoever thought you could stop taking the pill, carry on having sex and not fall pregnant, eventually? Damn stupid.

But Katherine was not registered with a doctor and, moreover, knew that abortions were illegal in France. She happened to know this because the right to a termination had, ironically, become something of a cause célèbre in France. Just before she had left Paris to spend Easter in London, the *Nouvel Observateur* had published '*le manifeste des 343*', a manifesto signed by some 343 women, all of whom admitted they had had an abortion. The feminist Simone de Beauvoir had written the manifesto, in which she maintained that a million French women had a dangerous and illegal abortion every year. The document demanded women's right to choose.

Katherine hadn't the faintest idea how to go about getting rid of her own unwanted creation but, equally certainly, was not about to try and find some backstreet abortionist, even if she could work out how to find such a person.

After the initial panic, Katherine thought about the courses of action she could take – hot baths, alcohol, excessive exercise came to mind. No one approach seemed direct or reliable enough – so Katherine did nothing but wait and hope.

As it turned out, her period came on during the weekend. Katherine could not tell whether this meant she hadn't been pregnant after all or if she had, indeed, been pregnant and lost it. If she was honest with herself, she didn't care one way or the other.

Her relief was tempered by the awareness that her own risky behaviour had created, at the very least, the possibility of what could at best be described as a tricky situation. While in Paris, sex would have to be off-limits. Once back in England, confident that she could now avoid putting on weight, she would re-enrol at the clinic and go back on the pill. It was that simple.

34

Je vous aime

Max managed to persuade Katherine to return for one last session. He had waited patiently outside the lycée at midday on Wednesday and, over several cups of coffee in the Bar Reynaud, he explained to her how close he was to completing the painting, that he'd never try to kiss her again, it was all a shocking moment of madness, he really and truly needed her presence just once more, he was so sorry if he had offended her.

'Enough,' said Katherine eventually. 'I'll come tomorrow after school – and then that's it.'

'Oh, thank you. Thank you, Katherine. I don't know how I can repay you.'

'It's pretty obvious – finish the painting,' she replied.

As Katherine climbed the stairs up to the studio, she kept asking herself why she had agreed. Why couldn't she just have said no? Did Max really need her for another session? What if he tried to kiss her again? Was she secretly hoping he would?

Max waved her in, as he busily sorted his brushes, adjusted the easel, and fussed over the exact placement of his tubes of oil paint. Anything rather than look at her directly. Katherine walked over to the seat where she usually posed and waited.

Eventually Max looked up properly and their eyes met. Keeping his voice as steady and matter-of-fact as he could, he asked if she wouldn't mind resuming the pose from the previous time, including, of course, the yellow scarf and the sheeting.

'I said I would, didn't I?' she replied and moved behind the screen to undress and re-emerge, carefully holding up the sheet around her until she had sat down, at which point she let it fall away behind her to reveal her shoulders and back. She turned her head towards him, mimicking exactly the pose he had insisted on before – and Max took up his brushes and palette. For the first 30 or 40 minutes he worked in silence, laying on the broad couches of colour, scraping back and re-layering. When he knew what he wanted to achieve, Max could work quickly, even using oils. He enjoyed the physicality of working wet on wet and the way that scraping back changed textures and the depth of colour. He knew that finishing the painting would take much longer than this last sitting but he was determined to capture those key elements that depended, in his mind, on having Katherine there in front of him.

Katherine's neck was beginning to ache and she shifted slightly on the seat.

'Do you need a break? I've got some coffee on the stove,' asked Max.

'Please, I'm starting to seize up. '

Max put down the palette and filled two small cups from the coffee-pot – very black and thick.

Katherine wrinkled her nose at the bitter smell.

'Sugar?'

'Of course, of course. Here you are.'

Two spoons of sugar took the edge off the bitterness and Katherine drank the coffee gratefully, cradling the cup in her hands. Handing it back carefully, while holding on to the front of the sheet, Katherine smiled at Max for the first time that day – and he smiled back.

'Friends?'

'Friends.'

Max put the cups back next to the stove and the two of them resumed their respective positions. Katherine, noticeably, more relaxed; Max, possibly even more tense than before, aware of an unbidden bulge in his trousers. He could feel his pulse racing and his hands were clammy. It was alarming how he reacted to this girl; he needed to focus on the canvas in front of him and fight against the terrible desire to take her that very moment, in his friend's studio, and to hell with the consequences. Max picked up his palette and set once more to work.

Perhaps an hour passed before it was evident that Katherine could not hold the pose any longer. The sun was beginning to dip down behind the rooftops and the light was fading. The final session was over and Max would have to carry on with what he had.

Katherine put on her clothes and carefully folded the yellow scarf, putting it down on the bentwood chair where she had until five minutes ago been sitting for Max.

'There,' she said. 'I'm leaving the scarf there – and you can pretend it's me while you finish the painting.'

'I'll think of it as my lucky token, then,' replied Max, going along with the deliberately inconsequential conversation.

Katherine turned at the door and held out her hand. Max took it and held her gaze, '*Je t'aime, tu sais,*' he mumbled.

Startled, Katherine withdrew her hand and said, as levelly as she could, '*Je vous aime bien, Max.*' And with that, she turned away, leaving behind the artist, contemplating the suddenly empty studio and the flat, lifeless scarf on the chair.

35

Out with the old

Terri was beginning to tire, just ever so slightly, of her liaison with Patrick. His friends were amusing, he took her to interesting places and he knew a lot about a lot of things. All of these good points, while adding to Terri's own fund of knowledge, were somewhat counterbalanced, she recognised, by his age and by his drinking.

Patrick, when clothed, was an attractive man. Unclothed, he was an old man. His long, lean frame, which made him such a good clotheshorse, looked almost emaciated close up. His very pale bottom and the tops of his thighs had a strangely wrinkled appearance – like a desiccated albino prune. His pubic hair was sparse and grey; his chest and shoulders were surprisingly narrow for a man of his height; when he lay on top of her, she could feel his hip-bones digging into her. None of this was calculated to arouse passion.

It was galling to have to admit that Katherine had been right to question the sense of moving in with someone old enough, at least technically, to be your grandfather.

But Terri could have accommodated the lack of physical attraction if all else had been perfect. At first, she hadn't taken much notice of Patrick's drinking. She was too busy enjoying the socialising and the intellectual challenge of keeping up with someone who could quote at will from almost any thinker or writer of note. Patrick was particularly fond of quoting or misquoting Kierkegaard – life can be understood backwards, but you must live forwards – or – you must have the courage to doubt everything – or, again – the important thing is to understand yourself, find the truth that is true for you.

If such aphorisms seemed revelatory at first, Terri had become frustrated by what she felt was Patrick's convenient way of avoiding what he himself really thought by quoting others. Not that Patrick tended to do this in company – then, he was quick to express an opinion, counter others' arguments or make clever witticisms. He could be the life and soul of any party – but once they were alone, he was more introverted, less willing to engage in normal conversation – and, when working on his translations, would brook no interruption. As a consequence, Terri had spent many hours devouring the books on Patrick's tightly-packed shelves. Among these, there were, naturally, several tomes on or by Kierkegaard and Terri recognised Patrick in the description of the man who would be the life and soul of the party, only to return home feeling suicidal.

Patrick was, at his heart, a deeply depressed soul. His experiences had undermined his once-held belief in the fairer, better world that would emerge after the second world war and had shown to him that, even in the realm of the personal, you could not defeat those in authority. His disillusion and great unhappiness had coincided – and he had turned to drink as the one sure solace.

In the early 1950s, Patrick had gone to work at the United Nations as a translator/interpreter. There, he found that politicians and diplomats would say one thing in private, something quite different in public. The functionaries were only too happy to shuffle papers, produce lengthy reports and shelve findings of any true consequence – all in exchange for inflated salaries and the undoubted comforts of life in the States.

He might have borne all this had he not fallen in love with the only daughter of the governor of one of the Southern states. They had met at a cocktail reception hosted by the UK's UN representative. Bored beyond measure by the meaningless small-talk, Patrick had been on the verge of leaving when his eyes fell on a slight, fair-haired girl standing awkwardly to the side of a small group of older men and women engaged in a lively conversation, punctuated from time to time by outbursts of loud laughter. Patrick made his way towards the girl and said, 'You look like you need rescuing; may I fetch you something to drink?'

The girl lifted her wide, green eyes up to Patrick's face – and he was absurdly and instantly in love. The girl proffered her hand.

'What a good idea! Let me come with you – I've heard all of Daddy's stories before – and,' she added in a conspiratorially low voice, 'they don't improve on a fifth telling.'

'Splendid.' Patrick extended his hand, 'My name is Patrick Holgate and, for my sins, I'm a translator in this tower of babel. And you are?'

The girl shook Patrick's hand, 'I'm Madeleine Sharp – and that,' indicating with a sideways glance,' is my father, Governor Hampton Sharp.'

This was not good news – Hampton Sharp was known as one

of the least progressive governors, even in the South, and had been a leading light in the short-lived, segregationist Dixiecrat movement. Madeleine caught the change in Patrick's expression and added quickly, 'Please don't judge me by what you've heard about Daddy. I'm sure you don't believe in visiting the sins of the father on the daughter.'

Madeleine was, of course, right. Patrick laughed and said, 'Forgive me. I know you can't choose your parents.' This was deliciously undiplomatic language and Patrick was taking a risk. But he didn't care – the girl was captivating.

Over martinis and olives, the two of them exchanged views on the usual range of small-talk topics. They steered clear of the contentious issues of the day – Korea, communism – but rather focused on recent shows they'd attended, favourite films, the best restaurants in town. And, all the while, Patrick was becoming more and more convinced that he had found the one he'd been searching for all his adult life. Her green eyes held his gaze steadily and without guile, she laughed readily and musically, revealing dazzlingly perfect white teeth that would have graced a Colgate advertisement. Before she left him to re-join the senator who was impatiently motioning to her that they must go, she gave him her telephone number, scribbled quickly on a convenient paper napkin.

On almost every day of the next three weeks, Patrick and Madeleine either spoke to each other on the telephone or met up and visited art galleries, walked in Central Park, enjoyed cosy suppers in small local restaurants and fell in love. It was that simple – and, Patrick feared, that impossible. He could not believe that such a clever, beautiful, wealthy and very young woman could be in love with a middle-aged, world-weary European with limited prospects and limited income. But love him she did – and, foolishly, they made plans.

Madeleine was desperate to go to college – she hoped Bryn Mawr – and enrol in their social and political studies programme. As she had said at the very beginning, her father's views were not her own and she longed to get out of the straitjacket imposed by who she was – or, more importantly, who Hampton Sharp was – and discover the real world. The difficulty was that the governor had other ideas for his only daughter – and a college education was not one of them.

'You see, Patrick,' explained Madeleine. 'Daddy thinks that women should stay at home, produce children and act as hostess for their husband's business. He's insisting I come out as a debutante and get married off to some spoilt southern boy from the right family. He doesn't care what I want – and mother is too worried about not supporting her darlin' husband to help me fight him on this. But I know there's so much more to the world than staying at home and being the perfect ornament. I want to use my brain.'

Patrick nodded in agreement, while he ran through the ways they might be able to overcome the governor's intransigence and release Madeleine from a sterile future. The answer came shockingly fast.

'Marry me,' he said.

Madeleine's eyes widened in surprise.

'Then you can go to college, any college you want. We could even go to Europe and you could study there, if you prefer. I've been thinking for a while that the set-up here at the UN isn't really for me and I could earn a living translating while you studied. We could go to Paris – you'd love Paris – or London. Wherever you choose. Marry me.'

Madeleine studied her coffee cup intensely and for what, to

Patrick, seemed an eternity. Then, lifting her liquid green eyes to his, she said, 'Yes, oh yes, dear Patrick. That would be so fine. We'll have to tell Daddy and mother straightaway. '

It wasn't fine at all – Patrick knew that the governor would be very unlikely to give his blessing readily to such a union between his only daughter and a lowly UN functionary. Madeleine's parents had, moreover, been unaware that their daughter had been meeting Patrick, so busy were they with their own packed social and political agendas. But Patrick wasn't prepared for what followed. On being told the news, Governor Sharp ordered his wife and daughter out of the elegant hotel suite where the family was staying. Then, he turned back to Patrick and gave him a frighteningly clear ultimatum.

'I don't know what nonsense you've been putting into my daughter's head, sir, but, let me assure you, you will not marry Madeleine. You cannot imagine that I would allow my precious darlin' to marry someone old enough to be her father. Why, you're not even an American! You will go away and not attempt to communicate with her. We shall be leaving New York today and you will not see her again and you will not try to see her again. If you come to our home, I shall have you arrested for trespass. If you try to elope with her, if she tries to run away to you, I shall have her committed to a mental asylum – as she is clearly not in her right mind. Do I make myself clear?'

The governor had made himself clear though Patrick could scarcely believe the ferocity of the attack – or, indeed, that the governor would make good on the threat to commit Madeleine. Could he really do that? Would he? In one way the threat seemed so overly melodramatic that Patrick was inclined to dismiss it as some kind of bluff from a man used to getting his own way and momentarily thrown off kilter. But the expression on the governor's face said otherwise – this man meant business.

Patrick did not reply but turned away and left the hotel suite, outwardly calm but inwardly shaking. As he walked slowly through the hotel lobby – Madeleine was nowhere to be seen – he realised that he could not risk her future simply because he loved her. He would have to comply and not see Madeleine again. And the next day, he handed in his resignation at the UN and had returned to Europe within the week.

The way Patrick had told the story to Terri, he took the decision on the grounds that Madeleine was so young that she would inevitably recover from any heartache and, in any case, there was nothing he could do. Her life would work out, one way or another, and Patrick could have no part in it.

Patrick also admitted to Terri that on his return to Europe – Paris to be more precise – he suffered what could only be described as a mental breakdown, retreating to the room he had rented in a small hotel on the Left Bank and emerging only to buy wine, bread and cigarettes. For several months he had brooded inside his room, all the while eating into his savings, as he had neither the energy nor the inclination to seek out work. But this state of affairs could not last – and Patrick had sufficient self-awareness to recognise that, however badly he felt, he would eventually have to venture back into the world.

Fortunately for Patrick, he had some old friends in Paris who left him alone for the first weeks but then took it upon themselves to call on him at regular intervals, force him out of his personal prison to drink coffee in the local bar – and sober up – and suggest possible contacts for work. Their efforts – and Patrick's own dismay one morning on seeing the haggard, bleary-eyed face of the stranger in the shaving mirror – eventually paid off and Patrick began to take steps towards leading a more normal life.

He eventually gave up smoking completely on 11 February 1954 – a date he celebrated every year thereafter by buying a packet of cigarettes and ceremoniously setting it alight. He did not give up drinking – but he cut back overall, even enduring extended periods of abstinence before breaking the fast with several more glasses of wine than was wise. And he found work with a technical translation agency, which over the years would provide him with clients in almost every industrial and commercial sector – from car manufacturing to machine tools supply to pharmaceutical production.

For more than 10 years, Patrick continued to live in the same small hotel (he used to say later that he had paved the way for the Duchess of Argyll, who lived for so many years in the Grosvenor House hotel – though on a slightly different scale). But, when the hotel's owners decided to retire and sell the business, Patrick took the radical step of renting an apartment in the 16th arrondissement – and there he had stayed ever since.

So, by the time Terri arrived on the scene, Patrick's daily life had long followed an established pattern – letters and translation in the morning, a swim, walk or visit to an art gallery or museum in the afternoon and supper or drinks with friends most evenings. After Terri's arrival, the pattern did not change much – though there were fewer evenings out with friends as Patrick decreasingly felt the compulsion to escape from his thoughts once night had closed in. Instead, he delighted in introducing Terri to his ideas, recommending books, arguing about politics, simply preparing and eating a meal. The pain that Patrick still carried with him from his experiences in New York was on the way to becoming more of a dim memory than an ever-present reality.

But for Terri the novelty and excitement of being with an older, more sophisticated and worldly man was wearing thin. She was beginning to feel that she had soaked up enough information and knowledge, that she had exhausted her interest in experiments into the paranormal beyond the Iron Curtain (a particular interest of Patrick's), that she was somehow missing out on other aspects of Paris because she did everything with or for Patrick. And she knew that the relationship with Patrick would not (could not) survive her return to Oxford for her final year.

'Patrick, will you miss me when I've gone back? ' Terri asked one evening. 'Because I will have to go back in a few months' time and I think we should sort of prepare ourselves for that.'

'How do you mean?' replied Patrick warily.

'Well, I think I should go back to living properly in the flat in Vincennes. Of course, I'd come over often and we could still do lots of things together – but it seems to me that we need to adjust to what's going to happen anyway – you know, get used to not having each other around all the time.'

Patrick considered the proposition. He'd always known that Terri's presence was a temporary joy. In many ways, he was astonished that she had stayed with him for as long as she had – astonished and flattered. Though she was not at all like Madeleine, she shared the youth and energy that Patrick remembered – and, while he did not love Terri, he was very fond of her and knew he would miss her company badly once she had gone. It made no sense to him for her to move away ahead of time and he realised that by making the suggestion now Terri was really saying it's been fun but I need to move on. He was not prepared to debate the point – in his experience, once a woman said she thought something should happen what she meant was this will happen.

'My dear, if that's what you would like to do, I'll not stop you,' he replied in an even if cool tone.

'That's fine, Patrick, but how do you feel about it?' asked Terri, seeking to assuage the small amount of guilt she was feeling about springing the idea on her lover.

'How I feel is not the point. It's what you want to do – so go ahead and do it. As you say, we'll still see each other – and you won't have to hang around with this old boy when you don't want to. It's fine.'

Patrick had not intended to sound bitter: he'd intended to sound cool, dispassionate, understanding – but it definitely came out as bitter.

Terri coloured slightly – Patrick was upset and he had also identified the underlying motive. She could be free to come and go as she pleased – see Patrick when she chose rather than be tied to him. No assuaging of guilt, then, but a grudging permission to leave. Terri was glad that Patrick was being so adult about it all – she could choose to ignore the pain he was feeling underneath. He was in effect helping her pack her bags.

The couple had one last evening and night together before Terri did indeed pack her bags and leave. Patrick drank the best part of two bottles of wine and fell asleep almost immediately after Terri had guided him to bed. For once she was rather glad that he had drunk too much – it avoided the embarrassment of what would undoubtedly have been a rather miserable fumble under the sheets.

And so it was that the next time Katherine called on Patrick, he was alone, nursing a large balloon of red wine and seemingly genuinely delighted to see her. Katherine had to acknowledge that the delight was mutual.

36

The price of success

It was the preview night for Max's show. Jocelyne paced up and down the apartment, her heels clicking impatiently on the polished floors. Max was locked into the bathroom, staring at his face in the mirror, steeling himself for the public exposure of his works. He had insisted on overseeing the hanging of the pictures and forbade Jocelyne to come to the gallery while the work was going on.

'I want you to see everything with a fresh eye,' he had told her.

'Max, do hurry up, you're going to be late for your own show,' called Jocelyne through the door. Reluctantly, Max turned the lock and stepped out.

'You look perfect,' he said. And he meant it – Jocelyne was dressed impeccably as always; her hair, newly cut and styled, cleverly framed her face, drawing attention to her brown eyes and delicately arched eyebrows. Gold and diamond jewellery glinted in the light as she moved. Perfect. Too perfect.

Jocelyne picked up her silk scarf, handbag and gloves and they left for the show.

Constance art gallery was down an ancient side street close to Notre Dame on the Ile Saint Louis. The gallery comprised two narrow, long rooms running from back to front, with the first floor room reached by a spiral staircase artfully inserted at the far end of the ground-floor gallery. There was another entrance via the old wooden staircase to the side of the rooms – but at shows this was blocked off visually, if not securely, by a red tape strung across the bottom step. That way, visitors were encouraged to stay within the confines of the gallery.

When Max and Jocelyne arrived, there was already a fair crowd of guests milling around the ground floor, glasses in hand. Some, heads bent over the catalogue, were dutifully inspecting each artwork – others were gathered in small, animated groups, drinking and chatting without apparently paying a great deal of attention to the art surrounding them.

Constance D'Albret, the eponymous gallery owner, elbowed her way out of one of the groups and grabbed hold of Max and Jocelyne with evident relief.

'At last! Where have you two been?' she exclaimed. 'Come along, Bernard Dumouliers has been asking to talk to you.'

Dumouliers was the art critic for *Le Monde* and did not usually grace with his presence what he considered minor shows of minor artists. So, his showing-up was something of a coup for Jocelyne and Constance, who had called in all the favours they could think of to cajole, charm or trick not merely Dumouliers but a host of other critics and collectors to the show.

While Dumouliers quizzed Max on his influences and on what he was trying to achieve with his latest oeuvre, Constance took Jocelyne to one side and whispered in her ear.

'Darling, I've already had two offers for the centrepiece – but Max told me very firmly when he brought it in that it wasn't for sale. Can you bang some sense into him? As you know, his work isn't flying off the walls – and now I already have two buyers. Who knows how many by the end of this evening? Let alone by the end of the show. We might even break even!'

Jocelyne turned back to where she could see that Max was struggling to give Dumouliers the kinds of answer he was looking for – as with so many artists, explaining the art did not come easily to Max.

'Bernard, I'm afraid I must whisk Max away. You're not the only person wanting to interview him, you know. But, if you'd like to talk to him later, I'm sure we can arrange something.'

'Thank you,' murmured Max as the two of them pushed into the now rather dense throng of people.

'Max,' called out Patrick. 'What a marvellous show - and I can say that though we've barely seen three paintings yet! But what I have seen so far tells me you've truly made some kind of breakthrough. Just marvellous.' Patrick had already downed two glasses of champagne and was well on his way to finishing a third.

'You are so kind to say so,' replied Max, as he cast his eye over the press of people. Where was his muse? Where was Katherine?

'Are you looking for someone, Max?' This from the ever-observant Terri.

'No, not especially. But I thought you might have brought your friend – what's her name? Katherine?'

'Oh, she's here,' replied Terri brightly. 'I think she's talking to Yvette over there. I'm impressed you remember her name, Max. She must have made quite an impression.'

'No, not really,' stumbled Max in reply. 'But she has seemed to be round at Patrick's most times we've been there. So, I just assumed..' Max's voice trailed away and he reached out for a glass of champagne from a passing waiter.

Meanwhile, the subject of this unsatisfactory dialogue had indeed been busily chatting to Yvette, who had recently returned from a tour of north Africa where she had fallen in love with the colours, light and shapes to such an extent that she was already planning her return visit.

Katherine caught sight of Max and lowered her eyes. She had hoped to avoid the preview night but Patrick – and Terri – had insisted on her coming with them and, given there was no good reason she could give to refuse, she had submitted to her fate. Turning her head away from where Max, Patrick and Terri were standing, she was surprised to see someone else she knew. Beatrice Duval was studying intently one of Max's paintings on the wall opposite Katherine while occasionally addressing a remark to her companion, a tall young man wearing a homburg and a bright blue waistcoat, his jacket slung casually over one shoulder. Beatrice herself was dressed in a long, brightly coloured kaftan and her hair tumbled over her shoulders in a cascade of Renaissance curls.

The word posers came unbidden into Katherine's mind, which may have explained her air of slight embarrassment when Beatrice turned and looked straight at her. Beatrice's own face registered a degree of surprise.

'Why, Katherine,' she said as she made her way towards her. 'How nice to see you here.'

'Hello, Beatrice. Are you well?' Katherine couldn't prevent the tone of formality in her voice.

'Absolutely. And you? Do you know Max? I didn't know you moved in these circles. What do you think of his work? I really like this one,' Beatrice pointed at the painting she had just left. 'Such a great use of colour. Don't you think? Max used to give me drawing lessons, years ago. Funny how life moves on isn't it? I don't think Max was very impressed with me as a ten-year-old but we're great pals now.'

Beatrice's capacity to talk non-stop had not diminished – nor her ability to centre the conversation on herself.

Katherine sighed inwardly but replied brightly enough, 'I know Max quite well, actually; he's great friends with Patrick – the tall man over there. And Patrick and my father go back to the Dark Ages!'

Beatrice muttered something on the lines of how interesting and drifted away, male companion in tow.

The press of people on the ground floor was beginning to ease up as people made their way upstairs to the upper gallery – and a few were returning to the lower gallery, a number of them seeking out Max. Katherine caught the odd word or two of the enquiries being directed at the painter. 'Who is she?' and 'Real or imagined?' 'Why so much yellow?' and similar phrases drifted through the hubbub. Instantly, Katherine realised they must be talking about her portrait; she also realised that she could no longer put off taking a look.

When she reached the top of the stairs, Katherine had a clear view down the gallery to the end, where a single large painting hung in magnificent isolation. The foreground of the work – the centrepiece of Max's show – was taken up with the portrait of a young woman as seen from the back, her head turned so that her eyes met onlookers straight on. Her bare back was suggested in a few deft strokes as was the slender curve of her neck. A few strands of fair hair drifted over a bare shoulder. A scarf hung limply over the back of a chair in the top right corner – the perspective making it seem as though it were a good 20 metres or so away in the far distance. Apart from the eyes, all the other pigments were variations on yellow and black – yellow walls with evenly spaced black circles; ebony-black chair; bright yellow scarf, with black fringing. The eyes were heavily outlined in black and their pupil centres were jet black and dilated.

It was quite unlike any other paintings by Max that Katherine had seen – uncluttered, spare – and, in her view, the better for it. She was relieved to note that nobody would easily identify her as the girl in the picture. But, that relief was short-lived when she began to look at the long series of smaller works that lined each wall leading down to *Study in yellow and black*. There were sketches in pencil or pen and ink, watercolours, individual studies of a shoulder or an eye and some experiments in colour-mixing showing yellows overlaid with blacks and blacks overlaid with yellows – some with colours dripping into each other, others with fixed blocks, rather like a colour card for household paint.

Anyone who knew Katherine would recognise the features of her face as presented in these smaller works or, indeed, would know her from the quick sketches showing a complete figure, dressed in jeans and a loose-fitting shirt.

Katherine felt betrayed. Max had promised that no-one would know the identity of his sitter from the completed painting. And to be scrupulously fair, that was true. But not being identifiable in the main work did not make up for being so clearly the subject of all the preparatory sketches. It could only be a matter of a few moments before Jocelyne made her way up the stairs and then, Katherine was fairly certain, all hell would break loose. It wasn't just Jocelyne, either – the other people who knew her would soon be upstairs as well. The sheer embarrassment of it all. Katherine shrank back into the corner; maybe she could slip away unnoticed, once the stairs were clear.

Soon, the second wave of guests was coming up the stairs,

including Max and Jocelyne in the company of agents and critics. As with most people before her, Jocelyne's attention was immediately drawn to the large portrait at the end of the gallery. She walked up to within ten feet of it and considered it intently. A slightly puzzled expression played over her face as she took in the yellows and blacks, the chair and the girl's face. She turned to look enquiringly at Max – and then began to take notice of the multiple sketches lining the other two walls. The puzzled expression rapidly changed.

'It's that girl,' she hissed at Max. 'No wonder you didn't want me to see it.'

Max could think of nothing useful to say so he simply shrugged his shoulders.

'Isn't it wonderful,' purred Constance at Jocelyne's side. 'You can see why we've got so much interest in it already. You really must persuade Max to let me sell it.'

'Oh yes,' said Jocelyne grimly. 'Quite extraordinary.'

Casting her eyes over the crowd, Jocelyne spied Katherine in the far corner. Their eyes met briefly – Katherine's wide and worried, the proverbial rabbit caught in the headlights, and Jocelyne's narrow and steely, sharp enough to pierce the strongest armour. The look lasted a matter of seconds before Jocelyne turned her head away.

Katherine had no time to plan an escape route because Beatrice and her in-tow companion were bearing down on her from one direction – Patrick and Terri from another. Both couples with the same question on their lips.

'Katherine! Why didn't you tell us you sat for Max?'

And, from Terri, 'Did Jocelyne know?'

'Oh, it was just one of those things that seemed a good idea at the time. And, anyway, if there weren't all the sketches, nobody would have known from the actual painting.'

'So, Jocelyne didn't know, then,' surmised Terri.

Katherine shot her a look but didn't comment.

'Still,' Terri carried on, 'all those yellows and blacks. Just like Yvette said. Who else could it have been?'

Damn Terri's memory, thought Katherine.

By this time, quite a group had gathered round the inner circle of friends, all keen to talk to 'Max's muse'. But the muse was in no mood for chat with strangers and, as politely as was possible, she extricated herself from the knot of people and made determinedly for the spiral stairs. Not knowing the gallery, she didn't realise that she could have pushed open the central door and made her escape far more easily via the building's staircase. But Max - on seeing Katherine leave - broke away from the crush around him and sprang through the middle door and down the stairs to catch Katherine before she had had time to leave the gallery.

'Why are you leaving?' asked Max, blocking the way to the street exit.

'I think you know,' replied Katherine. 'You've put me in an impossible position.'

'You don't understand, Katherine. I had no choice. Constance came over to catalogue the works – and when she saw the sketches, she insisted we include them. To show the evolution of the idea. And I could not think of a good reason to say no – because, after all, it makes sense from an artistic viewpoint.'

'What about the personal viewpoint? My viewpoint? You could have said the model wanted to stay anonymous. You could have said your finished work stood on its merits. You could have said anything – she couldn't force you.'

'Maybe, maybe not – but if I hadn't agreed, she might have called Jocelyne and then who knows what might have happened.'

Katherine looked at Max and felt something akin to pity for this grown man who looked strong but was in reality weak and cowardly in face of the much more forceful women who apparently ruled his life.

'Well, you were just putting off the day of reckoning. Lucky for you so many people seem to like the show – maybe Jocelyne will be able to get her money back – before she kicks you out.'

So saying, Katherine pushed past Max and through the open door into the muggy street air.

37

Peaceful protest

When Katherine found herself outside the gallery, she turned left and made her way towards the Boul' Mich. It wasn't a conscious decision – she merely wished to get away from the gallery as quickly as possible – so the direction she chose was purely accidental.

Crossing the Quai de la Tournelle, she turned right up the Boulevard St Germain. The avenue seemed unusually quiet but as she moved closer to where St Germain crosses St Michel, she noticed that there were small groups of riot police, CRS, lining the street.

Although it was nearly three years since the troubles of 1968, Paris had continued to maintain a semi-state of alert. An armed policeman, rifle at the shoulder, stood perpetual guard, for example, at the corner of the Rue de Rivoli and the Place de la Concorde. And on the Left Bank an armoured police car was in equally permanent attendance.

Katherine had seen the CRS once before, a small group of them huddling near the Place de la République in tense anticipation of possible trouble during a demonstration about wages. She had had to walk past this group of men, some of whom were slowly beating their batons against heavily-gloved hands. She had sensed their pent-up energy, like hunting dogs straining at the leash. And she had gratefully moved away, glad not to be involved.

It was a commonly-held view among those in Katherine's circle that the CRS were little better than licensed thugs – a fine line existing between law enforcement and criminal violence. So, Katherine was more than a little concerned when she realised that the groups of anti-riot forces could only mean one thing: there was a demonstration either already in progress or about to take place. And she ran the risk of finding herself caught up in the middle.

Looking up towards Place St Michel, Katherine could see that a crowd was slowly advancing in her (and the CRS's) direction. So, there was a demonstration, presumably heading for Place de la Bastille. As the line moved closer, Katherine thought she recognised vaguely one of the young men shouting at the front of the demonstrators. It was Halit, the Albanian whom Katherine had met at Josette's and Ann-Marie's flat all those months ago.

Katherine watched cautiously as the crowd passed by, hoping fervently that Halit would neither notice nor recognise her. Complaining about Albania's plight was not something she wished to become involved in, however tangentially. Naturally enough, Halit was too focused on his slogan-making and leading the 300 or so followers to notice the young woman standing to one side. Katherine watched the crowd as it retreated down the boulevard and continued on her journey towards the Boul' Mich.

As she made her way, her thoughts turned back to the political demonstrations she had attended. One in particular came to mind, a sit-in at Schools – and, with the advantage of hindsight, she recognised how trivial some student concerns were compared with those of people displaced from their own country.

Even at the time, Katherine had realised that it was a mistake to take part but there had been nothing she could do about it. She had watched as students continued to pile into Schools and settle down on any spare piece of floor. The white-blonde, floppy-haired anarchist who seemed to turn up at every demo was balanced precariously on a windowsill, waving his over-sized black flag as though he were Marianne leading the communards.

It had proved surprisingly easy to gain entrance – the university bulldogs could only shout in vain at the crowd not to break in, threatening the miscreants with dire consequences once it was all over. The students had laughed in their faces and pushed forward, buoyed along by the chant of No Files!

Once the mad scramble to gain entry had finished and the last student was safely through the doors, they were banged shut and desks and chairs piled against them. People milled around wandering what to do next, others settled on the floor, talking animatedly to their companions.

Eventually, Harry Carson and Alison Pope, leading lights of the Young Socialists and, incidentally, both products of well-known public schools, had climbed up on to a couple of desks and yelled for some quiet. Several hundred faces turned expectantly towards their leaders.

'Well done, everyone,' shouted Harry. 'We've made it – and there's nothing the authorities can do as long as we stay in here. We won't come out until they agree to destroy our files.'

A big cheer went up around the room.

'Yes,' cried Alison. 'But if they do try to get us out with force, we'll resist with force.'

Another cheer.

A hesitant voice piped up from the floor. 'Don't you think we should vote on that?'

Alison glared down at the speaker. 'Well, yes, I suppose that would only be right. OK, what do you say? The motion is we resist any attempt to remove us from Schools. All those in favour?'

A sea of hands waved in response.

'Those against?'

A handful of people had raised their arms, looking around desperately in the hope of more support. Katherine was one of them.

'Carried.'

Katherine had sat back, alarmed at the thought that the sit-in could turn violent, hoping fervently that it would all be over soon. If only the university would give in gracefully.

Dave patted her knee. 'Never mind, it may not come to anything. Hungry?'

'Not really.'

'Well, let me know if you change your mind.' And with that, Dave had dug into his rucksack and pulled out a rather squashed length of French bread and a hunk of sweaty Cheshire cheese. He had then settled back, contentedly munching.

Katherine took out a bottle from her own bag and unscrewed the cap. The water tasted good.

It wasn't that she was a political animal, far from it. But Dave had been very persuasive about how wrong it was for universities to hold files on their students, when the students themselves had no idea what was in them or to what use they might be put.

'Can't you see?' Dave had argued when Katherine had raised doubts about joining in the demo. 'If anyone attends a rally or questions some college ruling, down it goes in the files – and then MI5 or the police can use that information to keep tabs on people or blacklist them and years later you won't understand why you haven't got a particular job or can't get a loan. And it'll be down to being branded as some communist or socialist troublemaker when you were a student – and that's just not right. It's an infringement of our civil rights.'

Although Katherine did not hold to the conspiracy theory of government, she agreed that people had the right to know what information was being kept about them and the university did seem to be being particularly evasive in explaining themselves.

'Look, the LSE and Birmingham have shown they won't put up with it and so must we,' had concluded Dave.

'Alright, I'll come,' Katherine had replied, reflecting that *No files* didn't have quite the same ring to it as *Solidarity with the workers* or *Vietnam for the Vietnamese*, but maybe this was a battle that students could actually win.

The sit-in had lasted nearly two days. No attempt was made to break it up by force but slowly students drifted out of Schools – tired, hungry, possibly fed-up with the regular pep-talks from their leaders. What had seemed exciting at the beginning soon seemed tedious and, once the authorities had sent a message that they were willing to discuss the issue, provided the occupiers left the building, rather pointless.

Katherine was among the earlier ones to leave. The vote on resistance had alarmed her and the inability of anyone apparently to be willing to compromise went against her instincts to back away from confrontation if at all possible. She had come almost on a whim. She had left determined to let others play at politics – though, as she now reflected, for people like Halit it wasn't really a question of playing, more like living.

The cafes were quite busy but Katherine managed to find herself a table on the edge of one of the larger ones and ordered an express. She wished she had a book or newspaper with her but she hadn't expected to be leaving the gallery by herself nor indeed to be wandering the Left Bank in her current state of mixed emotions. Staring at her cup of coffee, Katherine reflected on the evening's events. Max had betrayed her trust – that much was clear. But what had she expected? That the sitter for his central piece could truly remain anonymous? That Jocelyne would never have the slightest inkling? And, then, did any of this really matter?

The painting was very good – in Max's words, it captured her essence. Katherine had to acknowledge that much. And Max may have tried to take their relationship further than she wished – but what was so bad about that? In a few months at most, she would have left Paris behind – and Paris, in turn, would quickly forget her. Max and Jocelyne would doubtless carry on as before, though, Katherine surmised, Jocelyne would keep an even tighter rein on her unreliable artist. Patrick would have his apartment and his bachelor life back – Terri had already made the important break and she herself would no longer need to book herself in for a bath and a meal. The girls at the lycée would have a new assistante – and she would no longer have to pretend to teach English to the insufferable children of an insufferable woman. All would be fine.

Katherine ordered another coffee. Would she really be fine back in England? There was no way she could talk about much of what she had done in the past year with her father or even her sister – Henry lived in his own dream world and Emily was, despite her best efforts to curb the tendency, extraordinarily judgmental. Jane was different; Katherine knew she could confide in her about anything and everything. But anything she told her would assuredly get back to Harry – and Katherine wasn't at all sure that that was a good idea, given his scarcely disguised interest in her.

Sucking on a sugar cube soaked in the bitter coffee, Katherine wondered what Penny would have made of it all. Strangely, she felt that her mother would have understood – but, of course, she could never know that for certain. But she did know that Penny would have held her close and stroked her hair, told her to look forward, not back. Two teardrops trickled down Katherine's face. She wiped them away, breathed deeply and drank her coffee.

38

The after party

By around 9.30, the crowd at the vernissage had thinned out to those directly involved. Constance had arranged an after-show meal at the Brasserie de l'Isle Saint-Louis for herself and her assistant Florence, Max and Jocelyne – so, after checking that all purchases had been correctly entered into the books and that the outside caterers had cleared everything up, Constance herded the small group out of the door. Earlier, she had asked Max whether he would invite his then unknown muse: he had replied firmly that that was out of the question.

During the short walk to the brasserie, Constance maintained an effective monologue on how well the vernissage had gone, how impressed the critics seemed to have been and how this was definitely the beginning of a brilliant second stage in Max's career.

'If the reviews are as good as I expect them to be,' she rattled on, 'I wouldn't be surprised to see some interest from the Americans. We could even be looking at an exhibition in New

York – I think I'll try and get hold of Ben Stanley from the Darco Gallery to see what he thinks.'

Jocelyne and Max walked alongside her in silence. Florence, struggling to keep up on absurdly high heels, tottered along at the rear.

At the brasserie, Constance was greeted warmly by the maître d' who ushered the group to a table next to a large mirror that reflected the lights of the heavy chandeliers made from barrels. The Isle Saint-Louis was an unpretentious, traditional brasserie, where the welcome counted for as much as the food – and the food was hearty and good value.

'I don't know whether we're going to eat very much, Guillaume,' Constance told the waiter, 'but we'll definitely start with a drink. We've got a lot to celebrate.'

'Champagne?' replied Guillaume. 'I can recommend the Billecart-Salmon.'

'What a good idea! We'll have that, please.'

'A toast to the show – and to Max, the toast of Paris,' Constance pronounced once all four glasses had been filled.

The four raised their glasses, Florence and Constance beaming broadly, Jocelyne managing a weak, thin-lipped smile and Max raising but then putting down his glass, untouched.

39

The morning after the night before

The sunlight filtering through the flimsy curtain on her dormer window woke Katherine early. And she immediately realised how much better everything seemed in the daytime. She had slept soundly once she got back from the Left Bank and, while the saucepan of water on the hob heated up for an infusion, she thought through the events of the previous night.

She remembered the conversation she'd had with Jane in the pub and her airy declaration that, if Jocelyne came to realise that she'd been sitting for Max, she would 'just have to deal with it'. Running away wasn't exactly dealing with anything – it was avoiding dealing with consequences. And she couldn't avoid everyone until the time came to leave. So, she needed to face up to the curiosity of friends and acquaintances, the undoubted ire of Jocelyne, the weakness of Max. And, you never know, it might actually be quite amusing to be thought of as the artist's muse, at least for a while.

Katherine knocked on the back door of the apartment and

was let in to take a shower. The maid who let her in was unusually friendly, 'Ah, it's you mademoiselle. They were talking about your art show at breakfast.'

They, of course, were the family – Beatrice had evidently graced them with her presence this morning, so eager had she been to spread the gossip.

Katherine showered quickly as usual and made her escape back upstairs. It hadn't occurred to her that the news would reach Mme Duval's ears. Certainly not that quickly.

By now it was well into the afternoon. Katherine decided to give Patrick a quick call from the café and find out if he was in so she could pop round. If nothing else, she wanted to make sure he didn't write to Henry about the latest art sensation, before she had decided whether and how to broach the subject at home.

But, stepping outside the massive doorway on to the Rue de Rivoli, Katherine found herself face-to-face with a tired-looking, distinctly rumpled Max.

'At last,' he said. ' You've come out. I was wondering if you were going to stay indoors all day.'

'How long have you been here?'

'Does that matter? I just needed to see you. Come and have a coffee with me.' Max pleaded both with his voice and his eyes.

They settled into one of the booth-like tables in the corner café and both ordered a small black coffee. Katherine played with the paper-wrapped sugar cubes, waiting for Max to say something.

'I am so sorry about last night, Katherine. Not sorry about the painting. It's one of the few works I am really proud of. But I am sorry I didn't tell you about the sketches and I should have realised how you would feel. Please forgive me.'

'And Jocelyne,' Katherine replied carefully. 'Did you explain to her that it was only a painting. That nothing else happened? Or has she thrown you out already? She certainly looked capable of that when I saw her.'

'No, no, of course not. She wasn't pleased, it's true,' said Max. Understatement of the century, thought Katherine.

'But you have to understand, Jocelyne was my inspiration years back when I was struggling to find myself as a painter. And now, well, she's hurt because I had to find the inspiration somewhere else – with somebody else.'

'Did you tell her you hadn't slept with your inspiration?' Katherine was surprising herself with the unusually direct control she appeared to be taking of this conversation.

'Actually, she didn't ask,' admitted Max. 'After the show, she was so tired that she went straight to bed when we got back to the flat – and I left before she woke up this morning.'

So, nothing had been discussed and nothing resolved.

'Well, I've decided I'm not going to worry about any of it. Life is too short and I've done nothing wrong. So, yes, you're forgiven. You should have warned me but you didn't – and you should have told Jocelyne but you didn't. So I guess it's all up to you how it works out. I've only a few weeks left before I have to go back to London and I'm not going to let one painting get in the way of the rest of my time here.'

Max stared at Katherine, his eyes wide in astonishment – this girl was tougher than she seemed. Max also felt regret – regret that he had deceived her, regret that they hadn't made love, regret that they never would.

'You're right, you're right,' he conceded. 'and thank you for forgiving me. I'm glad you are being positive about everything. You know, it's not such a bad thing to be an artist's muse.' Max attempted a smile.

Katherine's tense back softened, just a little. This was, after all, what she had concluded herself not so many hours ago.

'Maybe so,' she said. 'My fifteen minutes of fame.'

'Perhaps a bit more than that. Though less than if you'd been Mr Warhol's muse,' replied Max, showing he recognised the reference – and by so doing somehow making them both complicit in a private joke.

'So, where do we go from here?' asked Katherine eventually.

'Where would you like to go?'

'No, no, I mean what's going to happen now? You need to sort things out with Jocelyne for starters.'

'Yes, yes, of course. She'll understand, I'm sure she will,' Max said without conviction.

'Mm, I hope you're right – but, as I said, it's your problem not mine. I just want to be able to see Patrick, without having to worry if Jocelyne is there. It's bad enough having my landlady's daughter blabbing all about it – I don't think Madame Duval has much of a sense of humour – or much understanding about art, come to that.'

'You mean Beatrice? I tried to give her some lessons when she was small, you know. No talent for drawing and as spoilt as the rest of them – but she has quite a good eye for texture and colour. I wouldn't worry about her – or her mother.'

'And you're right – Celine Duval has no understanding of art. But, then, what do you expect from someone whose sole interest is her social standing.'

There was an edge of bitterness in Max's voice; Katherine wondered briefly whether there had been something more between Max and Madame Duval. But she dismissed the thought as quickly as it had surfaced.

While the café hummed around them, the artist and his muse fell silent. Neither knew what further to say to the other.

'I should go,' Katherine said eventually. 'Perhaps we'll see each other at Patrick's some time.' She proffered her hand as she rose from the table.

Max took the hand between both of his and stood up, his dark eyes focusing on the hand and then looking at her face, unwilling to let go, unable to say anything coherent.

Katherine shook herself free.

'Goodbye, Max.'

40

Fifteen minutes

The reviews of the show came out on the Monday after the vernissage. Critics agreed that Max had re-established himself as an artist to watch; his centrepiece, in particular, had caught the eye and also raised questions about his model. Many compared Max's earlier triumph and the role played by his then muse, the well-known arts patron and style icon, Jocelyne Perrault, with his new works, whose central subject was clearly younger and certainly far less well-known. Dumouliers of *Le Monde* pointed out that even the gallery owner Constance d'Albret did not know the identity of Max's sitter.

'That won't last,' thought Katherine as she read the review over a coffee in the café near school. Beatrice, if nobody else, was sure to unmask the sitter's identity.

And true enough, the very next day, a short piece on Page 4 revealed that 'sources close to the artist' had revealed that the model for *Study in yellow and black* was a teaching assistant at one of Paris's better-known lycées. The sources understood the sitter wished to remain anonymous.

Madame la directrice of the school sent word to Katherine that she wished to see her at the end of the morning.

'Mademoiselle Stewart, I have asked to see you because I am given to understand that you may have been posing as an artist's model.' The way Madame la directrice expressed this made it sound as though Katherine had committed more than one cardinal sin.

'Yes, Madame.'

'Well, is this true or not?'

'I did sit for an artist friend, Madame, and I believe the critics think the work is one of his finest,' replied Katherine. 'Do you have a problem with this?'

'The quality of the painting is not the point, Mademoiselle. It can only be a matter of time before our name appears in the press – and we cannot have reporters coming here and asking questions.'

'Well, Madame, I cannot imagine that the press will be interested for much more than a day or two. There are far more interesting things to report on. And, anyway, term is nearly over – and I shall have gone back to London very soon. So, I don't really understand what you expect me to do.'

Katherine was surprising herself by her cool reaction. She wished Jane could see her now.

Madame la directrice was similarly surprised. She was not accustomed to being contradicted by members of staff – or girls – and she had to think carefully before replying.

'Mademoiselle, what you say is undoubtedly true. However, I am extremely disappointed that you thought it appropriate to sit as an artist's model without consulting the school. This is not the sort of behaviour we expect from our staff.'

'I can only say I'm sorry you feel this way, Madame. But what I do in my spare time is, I believe, my concern. So, if there is nothing else, I have some recordings to make for Mme Grondin and I should not like to be late.'

And, so saying, Katherine left the directrice's study and headed, not to the language lab, but to the cloakroom, where she leant over a basin, breathed in and out very slowly and then splashed her face with cold water. Looking up at the mirror, Katherine stared long and hard at her reflection. She certainly had changed during her time in Paris.

41

Looking forward

Though Max's appearance had diverted her from going to Patrick's on the Sunday, Katherine did call in on him early that Tuesday evening.

'Well, hello, muse of the arts,' was Patrick's unusually cheerful greeting. The half-empty bottle of Bordeaux may have contributed to his jocular state. 'How have you been coping with all the fame and adulation?'

'Oh, please don't tease, Patrick. I'm certainly not famous and I haven't noticed too much adulation. Rather the reverse, actually, as I was called in by the directrice and given a real ticking-off – for bringing the school into disrepute. Or something along those lines, anyway.'

'I can well imagine,' Patrick replied. 'The Lycée Marie Crous prides itself on turning out doctors and lawyers, not artists' models. But I'm sure it will all die down very soon; and Paris will move on to the next juicy story, as it always does.'

'Fine – but that's the whole point. It's not a juicy story; it's just a story about a painting and the fact that nobody knew who the model was. There was nothing juicy about any of it.'

'I'm not sure that's how Jocelyne sees it. She's called me twice, no three times, already – telling me I must have known all along and why didn't I tell her. And worse besides.'

'Oh dear, this is just what I didn't want to happen. The fact that I posed for Max really mustn't affect your friendships – nor, indeed, whatever's between Max and Jocelyne. I do hope he's managed to talk to her properly by now,' Katherine's voice tailed away: she was not confident that Max would have sorted out anything.

'Max communicates through his art not through his words,' was Patrick's unhelpful comment. 'I doubt very much whether he and Jocelyne are even speaking at the moment.'

Patrick looked at Katherine quizzically. 'So, how did it all happen? If you don't mind my asking. After all, I do feel some responsibility, having brought the two of you together so to speak.'

Choosing her words very carefully, Katherine outlined the chance meeting between herself and Max, the chat in the café – and Max's plea for her to sit for him.

'So, I sat for him a few times – and he did the final piece from the sketches he'd made. I didn't see the picture until the vernissage. And that's all there is to it,' she concluded.

'Really?'

'Yes, really.'

Patrick realised there was no point in pursuing his line of enquiry; the determined set of Katherine's face told him that this was all she was going to say on the subject. So, he changed the subject and asked what her plans were for the remaining few weeks of her Parisian adventure.

'Well, I really need to get back to studying Delacroix. There are loads of paintings I've not looked at yet – and it would be more than stupid not to have seen them before I go home. So, I'll be doing that – but I haven't thought about what else I should see or places I should visit. It's silly, isn't it? You spend months somewhere and only realise how little you've seen just before it's time to leave.'

It was true that Katherine had begun to realise that she had yet to scratch the surface of the City of Light. There were, indeed, so many places she had not yet visited. From the catacombs to Père Lachaise cemetery and a myriad sites between. She resolved to make a list when she had got back to her chambre de bonne.

'Well, you can't do everything,' Patrick answered. 'I think you should look out for those spots that make Paris so very special for Parisians rather than just the sites that all the tourists go to.'

'Where do you suggest I start?'

'Just walking around you'll find unexpected gems – but I suppose the Buttes Chaumont park is up there on the list because it's so unlike the other public spaces, such as the Tuileries or the Luxembourg. To begin with it's rather hilly – and you can walk on the grass. It's more like an English park – lots of trees and some follies that wouldn't be out of place on a stately home's estate. An excellent spot to get away from the oppression of the city streets.'

Katherine was not at all sure that she found the streets oppressive but she also realised, as Patrick reached to re-fill his glass, now was not the moment to debate the point.

'Sounds great,' she said instead. 'I'll make sure to go there. And you're so right about avoiding the tourist traps – it's amazing what you can come across just by accident.'

As Patrick was evidently not going to invite her to supper, Katherine took her farewell, with a last rejoinder to urge on

Patrick the importance of Max's sorting things out with Jocelyne.

Outside in the bustle of the 16th arrondissement, Katherine briefly reflected that she might have done better to stay with Patrick and try, at least, to limit his alcohol intake for the evening. But, truth to tell, she wasn't in the mood to listen to other people's problems. She was only just beginning to sort out her own.

Once inside her little room, Katherine sat at the drop-down writing-desk and began to make a list, consulting her battered, red Plan de Paris book to help work out the routes between different places of interest. There were not quite five weeks left before she would have to return home – three weeks of term and two weeks that she had left free at the end to explore and take in the last of the city.

42

Cracking the code

'Colour is nothing if it doesn't suit the subject, if it doesn't heighten the effect of a painting through imagination.' As Katherine read this quote from Delacroix in one of the Musée Delacroix's free handouts about its exhibitions, past and present, she reflected on its relevance to Max's own painting of her. Did yellow and black really suit her, the subject?

What did yellow signify? The sun, obviously, and by extension a sunny temperament. Maybe that was what Yvette had meant when she said 'bright sunshine yellow'. Warmth? Brightness? Cowardice? Katherine thought of songs with the word yellow in them - the Beatles' *Yellow Submarine* and Donovan's *Mellow Yellow* came immediately to mind but that line of reasoning didn't seem much help.

What did she, Katherine, think of yellow? It seemed to her to be an optimistic colour, happy and associated with Spring above all else – daffodils, buttercups, dandelions. So, she felt safe in concluding that yellow was a 'good' colour.

But black? Darkness and death. Coal-black. A lack of light. Things hidden from view. The night. Mysteriousness. Bad humour or depression – wasn't it Churchill who had talked about the 'black dog'? Film noir – cynicism and violence. The list was not encouraging.

The combination of the two colours seemed to imply that, while she Katherine was open and straightforward on the surface, underneath the surface lay dark secrets or, at the very least, a hidden side to her personality.

She liked to think that as far as Max was concerned it was mystery that he saw in her.

Delacroix's own musings on colour seemed far more technical – how to enhance the effect of one colour by adding others. A dab of white here behind or next to another of brown or green; endlessly experimenting to produce the desired result. Katherine recognised the intellectual intent of Delacroix's quest and felt that she ought to appreciate better the paintings themselves. But, she had to admit, by and large Delacroix did not 'sing' to her – and she couldn't see how his use of colour was 'heightening the imagination'.

Revisiting his paintings in the Louvre, Katherine decided she needed to take just one picture at a time and really study it, for hours if necessary, in the hope that she'd be able to find a key to unlock her own lack of appreciation. She remembered what Max had told her during one of their discussions at his friend's studio, 'When you look at a painting – any work of art – there are two approaches you can take. You can admire the use of colour or the clever way the eye is led through to the heart of the scene or how brilliantly the sculptor has manipulated his chosen material. But what you need to do first, you must let the work touch you at a deeper level – aim to understand it in its totality. You can dissect it afterwards, if you need to.'

Katherine dutifully stared at the painting – one of Delacroix's most famous works. It was a large picture – like so many by the artist – maybe 10 feet by, she estimated, eight. In the centre of the painting was a sturdy young woman; her breasts were bare as was the one visible foot, and she was holding the French flag in one hand and a musket fixed with a bayonet in the other. On her head she wore a cap, which Amanda recognised as similar to the cap worn by Marianne, the symbol of the French Republic that adorned postage stamps.

Dead bodies lay in front of Liberty and behind her and to her side were people brandishing weapons. Closer to her there were three main figures, including a young boy with two pistols – and at her feet an older woman who might have been pleading with her or might have been gazing at her in awe: it was difficult to tell.

Most of the painting was dark in shades of grey, brown and blue – but behind Liberty was an aura of brightness created by clouds of smoke and the light fell on her face, which was turned in serious profile towards two very different-looking revolutionaries to her right. The red of the tricolour flag that Liberty held aloft was shockingly strong in contrast to the other colours.

Although the colours were dark they weren't cold and conveyed to Katherine a sense of emotion, passion even. She let her eyes run over the painting, up and down, left and right, along the diagonals. The central area of the painting was formed by a clear triangle, with Liberty's flag forming its apex and the guns held by the two figures either side of her leading the eye along each side. There was power and determination in every standing figure (marching to freedomland, Katherine reflected) – and all were prepared to walk over the bodies of those who had been killed for the cause.

For maybe the first time, Katherine could feel that she was actually getting a sense of what it was that made Delacroix great. And how his use of colour and light really was integral to the emotion of the subject.

From now on, Katherine spent as much of her spare time as she could studying Delacroix's works. Her file was filling up with copious notes and reactions. And, as so often is the case, the more she studied, the more she understood.

43

If at first

Shortly after returning to Paris in January after her mother's death, Katherine had decided that her hair needed a cut. It was by then way below her shoulders and, on a good day, she was pleased to see it swing behind her as she walked. But she felt she was stuck in an unsophisticated rut – hair up in a ponytail or down. This contrasted unfavourably with the sleek coiffures of the Parisian ladies she saw pass her by in the street or indeed with the styles adopted by those she had met through Patrick. Jocelyne's hair benefited self-evidently from expert cutting on a regular basis – even bohemian Yvette's head of hair was a riot of artful, short curls.

So, Katherine plucked up the courage to go inside a salon that she passed almost every day on the way to or from the lycée. The receptionist looked up as the potential client came through the door, her expression the typical combination of raised eyebrows and a smile that stopped at the mouth.

'Mademoiselle?'

'I was thinking about getting my hair cut,' Katherine began. 'Do you have anyone available?'

'Let me check.'

The receptionist looked down at the appointments calendar and then disappeared through a doorway to the salon behind.

'You are in luck. Mr Antoine can take you now. Please come this way.'

Katherine found herself propelled into a small – some might say intimate – room whose walls were lined with mirrors in gilt frames and under each mirror was a washbasin with various tools and lotions set out in front of each on a marble shelf that ran around the room's perimeter.

'Solange tells me you would like to have your hair cut, mademoiselle. But is this wise?' Mr Antoine looked into Katherine's eyes. 'It is rare to have such a fine length of hair. And once it has been cut, there is no going back. I suggest we deal with the condition of your hair, trim it a little and give it the life it deserves. First,' he opined gravely while taking strands of her hair between his fingers, 'we really must deal with these split ends..'

'But,' began Katherine.

'No buts, mademoiselle. You will be delighted with the result; I assure you.'

Mr Antoine brushed carefully through Katherine's hair and then, taking a few strands at a time, he twisted them round into a tight ringlet which he held aloft. His assistant, who was called Veronique, brought him a lit taper, which he then ran the length of the twisted strands burning off the tiny whispy points of the hair. He repeated the process for what seemed like hours to Katherine, who was feeling increasingly trapped in an alien world where the dryness of a slightly burnt aroma was mingling with the damp of the sweet smell of lotions and shampoos.

Eventually, Mr Antoine pronounced himself satisfied with the burning of the split ends. Veronique then washed and conditioned Katherine's hair and combed it out for Mr Antoine, who snipped away at what seemed to be minuscule lengths of hair. Then the whole head of hair was blow-dried and primped and cradled in Mr Antoine's capable hands.

'There, mademoiselle, what do you think?'

Katherine looked into the reflection offered by the mirror held behind her head. Her hair was looking very bouncy, with a slight inwards curl at the bottom, framing her head and shoulders. It wasn't short but it was elegant.

'Lovely,' said Katherine. 'Thank you.'

'You must look after your hair better, mademoiselle. I suggest a return visit every month to keep it looking good.'

Katherine thought this very unlikely but made no comment one way or another. It was even more unlikely when she was handed the bill.

Once outside, Katherine was pleased to enjoy the reflection of her hair in the shop window as she walked along. But with every gust of wind the carefully, coiffed crown began to look less sleek and more untidy. By the time she was back in her little room, the hair was drooping and try as she might she couldn't coax it back into the perfection it had been just half-an-hour previously.

But now that she was on the verge of departure, Katherine resolved again to have her hair cut - this time as she wished, not swayed by any hairdresser's blandishments. She would not return to Mr Antoine, his supercilious receptionist and eye-watering bill.

She found a small but cheerful salon close to the lycée and explained that she really, really wanted her hair cut – modern, no frills. She had happened to find a picture of Jane Fonda in

Klute in a magazine – and she took this along to show the stylist, who agreed that a cut on those lines would 'suit mademoiselle perfectly'.

Katherine emerged from the salon 90 minutes later with the shortest haircut she had had since she was 12 years old. And she loved it.

44

Leave-taking

The school term finished and Katherine bade her farewells to the English teachers and to her pupils. Mme Grondin squeezed her hand affectionately, kissed her on both cheeks and said the school would cherish the many recordings Katherine had made, 'in your perfect English accent.' Mademoiselle Mercier shook her hand politely and wished her success in the future. Madame la Directrice chose not to see Katherine.

The girls in Terminale, who had seemed to learn so little during their classes, surprised Katherine by presenting her with a box of exquisite chocolates from Debauve & Gallais, a Paris institution dating back to 1800, while her favourite students in deuxième had decided that an album by Charles Aznavour would be a fittingly French gift for their assistante d'anglais.

'You must listen to Tout s'en va, tout se meurt', urged Joelle.

Saying goodbye to Patrick took somewhat longer. He invited her round for supper, for which he reverted to the pattern of their earliest evenings together and bought her a steak to cook.

As usual, the wine flowed freely and the chocolate came out of the kitchen drawer at the end of the meal. While Patrick sounded off about what it would mean for the UK to join the EEC – a move approved by referendum in France not much more than a month earlier – Katherine drank her small, dark coffee with just a tinge of sadness as she realised this would be their last evening together for the foreseeable future.

'Have you heard from Terri?' Katherine asked during a lull in the conversation. Terri had already left Paris to visit friends before going with them to the Crystal Palace Garden Party. Joe Cocker was set to appear – and Terri loved Joe Cocker. The fact that the Beach Boys were also scheduled to play was an added bonus.

'Not since she came to say goodbye a couple of weeks ago. I don't expect to hear from her until she's back at college – she made it clear that she'll be very busy during the summer.'

'True. I saw her briefly for a coffee and she told me that she was going to be on the road a lot. But I think she'll be up earlier than usual as she still hasn't found anywhere to live. I've opted to go back into college but Terri's not keen – she likes the idea of being a free spirit.'

This was possibly not the best turn of phrase to have used with Patrick – but too late now.

'Yes, free to come and go as she pleases – Terri's not one for being tied down.'

The brief conversation about Terri put something of a dampener on the evening and Katherine wished she had resisted raising the question at all. She stood up and made her excuses. It was late and she was aiming to be up early the following day; it had been a lovely evening and she couldn't thank Patrick enough for all he had done while she was in Paris.

'Don't mention it, my dear. It's been a pleasure. You will give my love to your father, won't you? And do tell him that I have been working on the changes he suggested to my book.'

Katherine had completely forgotten about the book and was quite surprised that Henry had, after all, both read and commented on it. She would ask her father what his true opinion of the work was once she had returned home.

Patrick and Katherine hugged each other and she went off into the night. Patrick opened another bottle of wine.

Taking leave of Madame Duval was a necessary evil. Two days before Katherine's return home, Madame sent word that she'd like to see her.

The maid showed Katherine through to the drawing room, inside of which she had been only twice during her time in Paris – the first time for the awkward interview and the second when Madame Duval had so grandly handed over the £50 note to buy *The Vivisector*.

'Well, Mademoiselle Stewart, you will soon be leaving us. I hope your stay in Paris has been fruitful.'

'It's been great,' replied Katherine, searching in her mind for something more interesting to say. 'My French has improved enormously and I've been able to see some wonderful art – and, of course, I couldn't have lived anywhere better placed for both the school and for getting around the centre. So, thank you for giving me that opportunity.'

This all sounded both stilted and formulaic but it would have to do.

'Indeed, I expect your French may have improved rather more than Yves' and Andre's English.'

'That may well be the case,' stammered Katherine, ' but then their English was already remarkably fluent.'

'Yes, yes. You know, I am aware that my sons can be difficult but really I should have appreciated knowing how infrequently they agreed to lessons. Still, too late now...'. Madame Duval's voice drifted away, as though she had started a conversation she didn't know how to finish.

'And what about all that nonsense with Max Kobor? I hope you've got that out of your system?'

'Madame, I don't think it was nonsense – in fact, it's something that makes even more sense now than it did at the time. Have you seen the painting? It really is very good, you know. But I don't expect that the question of being an artist's model will crop up again. It was just one of those things that happen almost by accident.'

'Mm, that is as may be but I think it is just as well that you are now returning to England and your studies. I must admit, however, that the painting is one of the best that Max has produced for quite a few years. I hear that several galleries now want to show his work, which is a big improvement on recent years.'

So, Madame Duval had been to see Max's show – and she was well-informed on what was going on in the art market. Or perhaps she was simply repeating what Beatrice had told her.

'I'm so glad,' replied Katherine. 'Max deserves it.'

Having largely exhausted matters of common interest, the younger and the older woman were both pleased to curtail the conversation. Madame Duval shook Katherine's hand – or more precisely extended her hand for Katherine to take in hers – and bade her farewell and good luck, with a final injunction to make sure she left nothing behind in her room and that she gave the concierge her key.

Katherine did not see Max before she left – rumour was that Jocelyne had whisked him away to a friend's house in Biarritz 'so he can recharge his batteries and get away from the press.'

45

Homeward bound

Katherine left Paris without fanfare or drama. With her trunk and larger case despatched some days earlier, she walked easily with her one small case to Châtelet, so she could take one last look at the buildings lining the now very familiar route along the Rue de Rivoli.

Instead of flying back, Katherine had decided to take the boat train to London. Time was not of the essence and a railway journey seemed more romantic and more of a real voyage than re-taking a student flight back to Ashford. She had splashed out on a first-class ticket to enjoy the full experience of this increasingly antiquated mode of travel. So, from Châtelet, Katherine took the metro to Gare du Nord and there boarded the train on which she would stay throughout the journey.

It was a long, hot and noisy journey - not particularly romantic after all – and Katherine learnt that it was almost impossible to sleep properly, especially when the train carriages were being chained to the ferry's deck. Moreover, the train arrived early at Victoria Station, which meant that it stopped short of the station and idled in a siding for nearly two hours before drawing into platform 2 and the bustle of a London morning.

Pushing through the crowds of travellers, Katherine could see Emily hopping up and down trying to find her sister. Katherine waved enthusiastically in her direction to catch her eye and Emily rushed forward to hug the returnee.

'You're back!' exclaimed Emily somewhat redundantly.

'Mais oui – I mean, yes. Thank you for meeting me.'

'What's a sister for if not to greet the prodigal one on her return? But what have you done to your hair?'

The two made their way to the Underground – darker, busier, noisier than Katherine's beloved Metro – and were soon back home, where Henry clasped Katherine firmly on the shoulders and kissed her on her cheek.

'I'm so glad you're back safe and sound. Let me just finish a paragraph or two and then you can tell us all about Paris.'

'Shall I make a pot of tea?' asked Emily. Henry and Katherine caught each other's eye – some things didn't change.

46

Year of revolution - 1989

Katherine settled back in her chair and poured herself a coffee. She had already taken her bowl of muesli from the fridge: prepared the night before, it was now lusciously creamy and indulgent in contrast with the strong, black coffee. The *TLS*, *Guardian* and *Times* were to her side on the table and she picked up the latter to catch up with the news of the day before she had to leave to give her first lecture of the week, *Is Romanticism definable?*

The radio, tuned in to one of the French music stations, was playing in the corner of the room. This particular station alternated modern hits with the classics and, to Katherine's delight, the distinctive tones of Charles Aznavour began to sing *Tout s'en va*, the track pointed out all those years ago by her pupils in deuxième. The verse beginning *Kate, Kate à l'accent que j'aimais* never failed, however momentarily, to make her pause and listen. She had, however, long ceased to worry about the implication that, despite her best efforts, she still managed to mangle her French.

As for the line that said she was essentially malleable, despite being English – well, that was for others to decide.

The biggest news in the papers and much of the editorial analysis concerned the official declaration of the Hungarian Republic by President Matyas Szuros, exactly 33 years after the outbreak of the uprising that led to the Hungarian Revolution. Communism in Hungary was dead; its new constitution allowed a multi-party system and free elections.

Reading the despatches from Hungary, Katherine reflected that she would never have met Max, the revolutionary turned artist, had it not been for the crushing of the rebellion in 1956. And then she remembered Halit and his impassioned speeches about Albania. She hoped that Albania too would soon go the way of the other Communist Bloc countries – freedom was in the air, an uncrushable force, it seemed, once Gorbachev had declared that the Soviet Union would no longer intervene militarily to support the failing Communist regimes throughout eastern Europe.

Katherine was smiling to herself as she turned the pages of the paper, composing in her head the message of congratulations that she would send to Max, who was, she knew, staying in southern France at Beatrice's retreat. Yes, Beatrice had done what she said she would and followed in the steps of Picasso.

But Katherine's mood changed when she turned to the next page.

The Times, 24 October 1989

The unexpected death of renowned artist Max Kobor has been announced by fellow artist Beatrice Duval, at whose home he had been staying while preparing for a major retrospective of his works in St Paul de Vence.

Ms Duval said, 'It is with a heavy heart that I must announce the sudden death of Max Kobor. Not only was he a great artist, he was also a very dear friend. May he rest in peace.'

A figurative artist who dabbled briefly in surrealism and then heightened realism before returning to his first love, the female form, Max Kobor became a leading figure in the arts scene in Paris in the 60s and 70s.

Born in Budapest in 1933 to parents of modest means, Kobor studied at the Academy of Fine Arts where he became a leading light in the student movement, which erupted into the Hungarian Revolution of 1956. A wanted man, Kobor managed to escape to France – one of the more than 200,000 Hungarians who fled the country.

Kobor made his way to Paris, where he earned a meagre living as a private teacher until a chance meeting with Jocelyne Perrault, a well-known patron of the arts. Madame Perrault became both Kobor's lover and muse, inspiring a series of acclaimed portraits that placed Kobor at the centre of the Paris art scene for several years. However, when Kobor began experimenting with a quasi-surrealist approach to his work, his many fans began to fall away and he struggled to find buyers for his works.

A second chance encounter with a young English student was to lead to Kobor's most famous work 'Study in yellow and black' (1972), which relaunched his career and led to major exhibitions in New York, Berlin and London.

Although Kobor and Mme Perrault parted company not long after the New York show in 1973, they remained close and it was said that Kobor never truly recovered from his grief at her death following a skiing accident in 1983. Beatrice Duval was instrumental in persuading Kobor to agree to a retrospective, scheduled for January next year.

The cause of Kobor's untimely death at the age of 56 has yet to be confirmed.

Katherine put down her cup and stared in disbelief at

the notice. Why hadn't Beatrice called her? What on earth had happened?

She knew that Max had been worried about the show. But that kind of emotional stress was part and parcel of being an artist, not something that should cause a heart attack, which seemed the most likely explanation.

Taking a deep breath, she dialled Beatrice's number.

The funeral took place one week later. Katherine flew out on Dan-Air from Gatwick a couple of days before and Beatrice met her at the airport from where they drove the 20 or so kilometres to Beatrice's Saint Paul de Vence estate. Despite only limited success in her artistic endeavours, Beatrice had been able to purchase the estate following the death of her father some years previously – he had left a small fortune to each of the children.

The funeral was well-attended by the great and the good of the French artistic world and a smattering of art collectors, gallery owners and journalists from other countries who also came to pay their respects to Max. There was no one from his family – his parents had died many years earlier and he had been an only child.

Two key figures were no longer around. Patrick had died nearly 10 years earlier, having lost his battle with his inner demons and with alcohol. And then there had been Jocelyne's death in an avoidable skiing accident. But Madame Duval, cool as ever, came for the funeral as did Yvette, who greeted Katherine warmly and hugged her close. 'You inspired Max like no other, not even Jocelyne,' she whispered.

Back at Beatrice's rambling country house, the drink flowed freely, accompanied by tray upon tray of beautifully presented canapés. Beatrice had spared no expense in saying goodbye to Max, to whom she referred loud and often as her former mentor. Katherine reflected that a few, private lessons from Max in her teen years scarcely constituted mentoring but, then, self-aggrandizement was something of a speciality of the Duval family.

'And how did you know Max?' asked the stranger standing next to Katherine.

'We met in Paris when I was a student in the early seventies.'

'Ah, so you were around when he painted his *Study in yellow and black*? Did you know the model?'

'You could say that,' Katherine replied, as she turned to the waiter for a second glass of champagne.

* * *